Underneath
Rockville

Underneath
Rockville

Raymond C. Wood

UNDERNEATH ROCKVILLE

iUniverse books may be ordered through booksellers or by contacting:

iUniverse
1663 Liberty Drive
Bloomington, IN 47403
www.iuniverse.com
844-349-9409

Because of the dynamic nature of the Internet, any web addresses or links contained in this book may have changed since publication and may no longer be valid. The views expressed in this work are solely those of the author and do not necessarily reflect the views of the publisher, and the publisher hereby disclaims any responsibility for them.

Any people depicted in stock imagery provided by Getty Images are models, and such images are being used for illustrative purposes only.
Certain stock imagery © Getty Images.

ISBN: 978-1-6632-1102-6 (sc)
ISBN: 978-1-6632-1101-9 (e)

Library of Congress Control Number: 2020920123

Print information available on the last page.

iUniverse rev. date: 10/15/2020

Preface

Rick and Tess Martin, a middle-aged couple, buy an old run-down dairy farm in rural Massachusetts near the Rhode Island border. With the help of their "twin sons," who are both carpenters, their beautiful daughter, and her husband; they planned to bring it back to its former glory. However, one night the twins went into the small town to see if there was any "action." Not knowing, the real action was underneath the ground ... waiting to recruit them!

Chapter 1

Rick and Tess Martin emerged from the "Nineteenth Century farmhouse" that they just bought for short money with their goal to bring it back to its former glory. It was once a dairy farm in rural Massachusetts, near the Rhode Island Border.

Rick grabbed his wife's shoulder as they were heading for their vehicle. "So, what do you think Babe?"

",Did we make the right move in getting out of Park City to the country?"

Tess, a forty-two-year-old former "financial secretary" for an insurance firm smiled. "Without a doubt hon. I know it's going to be a challenge, but I know we will bring the old girl back to when it was a milk farm." Rick said.

"I couldn't agree more. Just breathing the air here is enough of a reason to start a new chapter in our lives, and with our twenty-four-year-old twins, who are both carpenters, and our beautiful daughter and her husband wanting to pitch in, it's a no-brainer. Let's go into Rockville to get a bite to eat."

They got into the new Red Ford F350 Flatbed 1 ton and that Rick bought and dressed it up by changing the duel steel wheels to chrome after trading in the BMW as they drove down the long driveway.

Tess, a medium height dirty blonde, that has kept her shape over the years: always adhering to the standing gospel, of moving up in age doesn't mean you're going to lose your looks, you just got to work harder to keep it; laughed and said, "Honey, it seem so funny to you see you in coveralls, after wearing suits for years."

"Yup."

Rick, a salesman for a beverage company, thanks to his being savvy in the stock market, is now working part time. He grinned.

"And guess what Honey?"

"What?" Tess asked.

"These coveralls feel so good that I'm not wearing any underwear." "No way!" Tess laughed, "I don't believe you!"

"Oh yeah Babe, just put your hand on my crotch."

Tess reached her hand down, when she felt a torpedo waiting for take-off. "Oh my God! This country air has got a grab on you!"

"Shall I pull over dearest Tess?"

"Babe, when we get home to our old farmhouse bedroom, you're going to be one lucky guy!"

Chapter 2

They could hear the bell on the old converted town hall ringing for 12 noon.

"Well," Rick quipped, "There's three diners in the place, we have been to two of them, let's try Ben's Diner."

They pulled into the parking lot, then took seats inside that looked older than their farm house. The waitress took their order, when Rick noticed a man in a booth in the corner staring at them. The man suddenly got up, walking over saying, "Hi, folks. Sorry for staring at you. Aren't you that couple that bought the old Johnson Farm over on Chatham Road?"

"That we are." Rick responded.

The man, probably in his late seventies, with a scruffy beard, and had paint stains on his clothing, said "Did they tell you about a deep well somewhere between the back-boundary line and the old out house, that I'm sure by now is probably gone?"

Tess piped up, "No, we just know about the well on the side of the house." The man thought and curled his beard saying" That sounds peculiar."

"Oh, folks. I should introduce myself. Clarence Hopkins, most people call me "tobacco.""

It's a nickname I got from always chewing the stuff. I stopped a couple of years ago, and what's left of my old friends, say it's remarkable that I am still alive. Well, enough about me, my grandfather knew Gus Johnson, He had a nice operation, he was always a hard worker and had a good herd of heifers. He had a worker, a guy called, Parko. He was an immigrant that Gus had hired supposedly from Mexico. Quite a worker; this Parko kept things running smoothly. Then, one day he disappeared. Old Gus thought he vamoosed back to Mexico. It was probably a couple months later that workers looking for a wandering cow stumbled on to the well, and sure enough, they pulled the body of poor Parko out. They say it was covered up with plywood and overgrown with brush; that Parko unfortunately met his Waterloo." So, I thought I would warn you in case you didn't know. Of course, this happened sometime in the forties."

Rick called the waitress over for a coffee refill, telling tobacco to join them.

"Oh, thank you folks, but I'm all coffee'd out. Besides, I got to get the wife to give her a ride to afternoon bingo."

Tess gave him a big smile and remarked, "We really appreciate you telling us. Our sons will be over tomorrow, and we will see if they can find it." Tobacco tipped his hat and left.

"Damn," Rick came across, "These last owners probably didn't know anything about it, or they would have mentioned it."

Tess thought for a moment, then putting her thoughts into words, "You know how everything was just positive? Now this gives me a real uncomfortable feeling."

Rick sipped his brew saying, "Don't worry yourself none. Mark and Billy should be here tomorrow, and Cassie and Carson this weekend.

Chapter 3

The next day, while Rick was reading the newspaper, and Tess was preparing breakfast;

they could hear the rumble of Billy's Camaro SS.

"Hey, Rick," Tess called out, "Looks like they're in time for breakfast."

Billy, followed by Mark, were of course twins, but to their parents, they were so different. Both were twenty-four, of medium height, both with sandy blonde hair, with rugged frames, that climbing up roofs and working construction kept them lean, and the eye to many of the young women around the Park City area.

Billy smirked, "Hey Mark, I told you we would make it for breakfast." Mark reminded his mother he likes his bacon well done.

Tess laughed, "Don't worry yourself boys, I know exactly how both of you like your breakfast."

Rick matched Tess's laughter.

"Gee whiz guys, how do you think she would know that?"

After everyone had a hearty feed, Mark said, "It seems like in the country everything tastes better."

Billy spewed off, "That's because you're smelling the cow shit."

Mark came back with, "You're going to smell it all the time when I nail you to the house."

Tess put her hand up, "Come on hellions, be nice now, we've got plenty of repair work to do."

Billy chuckled, "Wow, you can almost see the light coming through the roof." Rick commented, "All the lumber is on its way. Two big loads, around 1:00pm."

Then he told them about the tobacco story. Mark, who was the adventurous one, was eager to start looking.

The lumber came a little after noon, and Rick, holding a blueprint, would tackle the renovations of the house Monday morning, with the two men hired from town to help.

So, Billy and Mark, hit the south meadow, while Rick and Tess covered the east side. Rick said, "Be careful, and call on the cell if anything looks like an abandoned well or something that was covered over."

After an exhausting two-hour search, no one came across anything remotely as a well, or evidence of one. Although, Rick did find a couple pieces of wood, that could have been a part of an outhouse. Then again, it seemed unlikely. It wouldn't have been disintegrated after all theseyears.

Returning to the house later, the twins went into Rockville to check out the "action."

Tess laughed, saying to Rick, "Hon, I don't know what kind of action they will find in this

"Well," Rick quipped, "You know our guys are as red blooded as yours truly."

Flexing his muscles, Rick continued, "Rockville, and the damsels, be ready for the "Martin Twins."

Tess laughed, "And you my love, the father of these hellions, get ready to be my hellion in chief." As she undressed him with her blazing eyes.

"What, now?" Rick smiled.

Tess curled her lips, "Did I stutter?"

Chapter 4

Spring.

The next day, the first Sunday in May, shone bright; and really the first warm day of the

Cassie and Carson pulled into the driveway.

Looking out the window, Tess could see the bright Silver Lexus pulling up. She greeted them as they stepped in, giving them both a hug.

Cassie, a stunning blonde with hazel eyes, a killer smile, and a shape that she keeps by long distance running; looked around, "Where is everyone Mom?"

"Oh, Dad is checking the lumber count that was delivered yesterday, and your brothers are still in never-never land. They went out on the town last night, and God only knows what time they got in."

Carson laughed, "Where in Rockville does anything happen? It looks like they shut the town down at 9 o'clock."

Cassie, who works for a lawyer commented, "Are you kidding Car, those hoodlums could party with the Pope."

Rick noticed the Lexus, while walking over he was thinking about how he's not very fond of Carson. In his way of thinking, a rich kid who was born with a silver spoon in his mouth, and somehow to him, perhaps only him, that he displayed a "fake love" to his lovely daughter. Walking in, the rugged salesman, who was also a union carpenter earlier in life, greeted Cassie. She gave him a warm hug, then Carson shook hands with Rick saying, "Hi, old man. Are you ready to rock and roll this afternoon? I can help out until Wednesday, when we got to get back to Park City."

"No problem."

Then thinking, does he really know how to use a hammer?

Finally, as the aroma of coffee and bacon fermented throughout the house, the twins managed to emerge from an upstairs bedroom. Red eyed and looking like they ran into a Mack truck.

"Oh my God," Cassie commented, "Where did you guys go?"

Billy throwing his shirt on, said, "You know sis, I don't think I remember."

Mark not as bad as his brother, pointed out they were at a bar on the edge of town and were caught up in pool, drinking, women, and a few arguments; not necessarily in that order.

Rick shook his head, "I told you guys about drinking in a small town. The cops would love to bag out-of-townees."

Marks eyes fluttered, "Yeah, no shit Dad."

They started coming after us when we left, but Billy had the Camaro in rocket take off, the cops never got close."

Billy exclaimed, "I did?"

"Yeah," Mark mildly blasted him, "You would've killed us both."

Seeing that his mother was really upset, Mark softened it.

"Well, maybe we were well out of their reach. They probably only saw the tail lights." Rick said, "Billy, on the side of precaution, the green shed beside the barn is empty. Park the car in there in case any cops come around." "Oh, come on Dad. I don't think …"

Rick cut him off pointing to the door.

Tess responded, "Billy, the country breakfast will be ready by the time you get back."

Chapter 5

Hours later, all were on the wrap around farmers porch, shooting the breeze, when a car came down the long driveway.

"Who could that be?" Rick questioned.

Billy jumped up, "Mark, it's those chicks at the bar. They were driving a blue Camry." Mark smirked saying, "This ought to be interesting."

The twins walked over to meet them as they drove up. Cindy Lou, the driver; a bright red head and a real party animal, stuck her head out the window.

"Oh, hi boys. One of you dropped this last night." Showing them a chain necklace with dangling skulls.

Mark said, "Billy, that's yours. It must have come loose when you were doing your crazy strip tease."

Billy thought, "Damn, I guess I really tied one on. I barely remember."

The girl in the passenger's seat by the window spoke up, "Do you remember telling us to come over to check out the farm?"

The third girl in the back, probably the same age as the other two; in their early twenties, said, "Do you guys want to take a ride with us?"

Cindy Lou looked at the porch, "Those your folks?"

Mark thought, these chicks are hot; no way we're not going to take a ride. Then they climbed in the back seat.

Billy commented, "A nice ride, with nice chicks." The back-seat girl Karen, a blonde, laughed. "That's not what you said last night."

"What do you mean?"

All the girls broke out in laughter. Cindy Lou reminded Billy, "You told us; nice chicks, nice racks."

Billy grinned, adding, "And I stand by that statement."

Everybody chuckled, and Mark could see the three were eating that up.

Tess looking, said, "A blonde, a red head, and one with jet black hair; our sons know how to pick them."

Cassie put her spin on it, "I just hope they don't get too hopped up on whatever they all plan to do. They might be missing in action tomorrow morning."

Rick kind of shrugged it off, "No, I think they know we're counting on them."

The blue Camry wasted little time as it traversed onto the rural main road. The olive- skinned girl with jet black hair who Mark really had the hots for, smiled at him; he suddenly remembered she was originally from Peru, and her name was Shara.

"So where are you kidnapping us to?" Billy said as he was ogling Karen's tight halter top. "You'll see," was Cindy Lou's reply.

The car turned up into a narrow dirt road, when you could hear the blare of loud music. Three good sized men around the twins age, were grinning and waiting with a sinister intent. Mark at once recognized them from the bar last night. The girls drove up and piled out rather abruptly. The twins slowly got out, Billy saying, "What's going on?"

The taller of the three, quickly approached Billy, slamming his fist into his stomach. Billy doubled over. Mark going to his aid, was tackled from behind and thrown down. The biggest guy called Red, who threw the punch was livid.

"You fuckin' out-of-townees making a play for our girlfriends, are going to be taught a lesson."

Mark put his hand up, "Hold on, we had a few drinks, were partying, not looking for trouble. Just drinking and smoking weed, just danced a few times."

Karen the blonde, put herself beside Red. "Honey, that Billy guy was trying to grab my ass," and Cindy Lou added, "They both were trying to get us out to the back of the bar to suck their cocks."

Mark knew that was a lie, because it never happened. Roland said, "Let's fuck up these creeps."

"Wait!" The Spanish girl interjected, "We were all partying, drinking, and smoking reefer.

No one did anything that I could see."

Cindy Lou got in her face, "Shara, shut up. You weren't even there. All you were doing was grinding the Mark guy."

"Oh, really?" Roland, Shara's supposed boyfriend exclaimed. "Come on, let's teach these scumbags what we do in Rockville."

Vern, a little more focused than the other two, yelled, "Quiet down. Two of us are already on probation. We don't need to maim anybody."

Red yelled back, "Shut the fuck up Vern. We're going to beat them senseless."

"No." Shara stood between the twins and Red, who pulled a golf club from his truck. For almost a minute it would go either way. Then Red threw down the club, saying to the twins, "This is a warning, we find your asses around town you're going to have broken heads."

The twins got in the back seat of Red's double cab pickup, as Red, Vern, and Roland quickly drove them to the head of the driveway. They warned them, saying they got off easy, and if they ever come near their chicks again they will be dead meat. Then, Red pulled out, what looked like a .45, threatening them with it.

Mark could see Billy had taken quite a wallop when Red sucker punched him. "You okay Billy? It looks like you got the worst of it."

Billy was beside himself, spitting out, "Those bastards aren't going to get away with this, and those double-crossing snatches. They led us to a trap, or should I say ambush!"

Mark followed up, "If Shara didn't get in the middle, we could have been beaten to death."

Billy disgustingly added, "That bitch Cindy Lou was all over me at the bar." "Ya!" Mark was seething as he walked to the house.

"I had some ideas about the Spanish chick, she never said she had a boyfriend."

"Ya," Billy reiterated, "Damn broads, they're so evil."

Mark thought, "Why would Shara get in the middle? Especially because of her Roland, her pocked-faced supposed boyfriend?"

The twins went in, took quick showers, and did their best to avoid any of the family who, for the most part, were watching TV.

The next morning, after breakfast, they all went to start on renovations. That first day, much was done, and after the hired help left, Tess and Cassie made a delicious meatloaf, that everyone enjoyed. Gladly, not much was said about the three young women, so the twins didn't offer any information.

However, for Mark, Shara was in his mind big time; and as his grandfather would say; "You're smitten." Although, Billy kept wanting to get revenge, Mark wanted just once more to talk to the soft-spoken Spanish girl, and it just seems inconceivable that she would team up with roughneck Roland, who seemed one step from half a brain. However, he doesn't know where she lives, only knows she likes to play pool at Jimmy's Bar.

Around the middle of the week, Mark told his brother his obsession to find the olive skinned, jet black haired immigrant from Peru.

Billy said, "Mark, that's not a good idea, to go to the bar. You know those assholes will jump you. You keep telling me to forget about revenge, but you want to go back into the lion's den." Then he laughed saying, "She had too many drinks, that's why she was pawing you."

Mark came back with a sour remark, "You're probably right, but I can't get my mind off her."

Billy thought, "Remember behind the bar, there was an access road that came near the back door?"

"What? I can't believe you remember that."

So, within a couple of weeks, the twins devised a new plan.

One of the hired help, a guy named Juan, whom Mark had gotten friendly with, "a lifelong townie"; who along with the other hired man Benny, would play poker with the twins after working on the farm project. Then one night after they broke off cards, Mark and Juan decided to smoke a joint, and for some reason, probably because he was feeling blue, he told Juan about the girl and what happened. To his utter surprise, both he and Benny knew Shara and the three boys whom he calls "bar room bums," but then again, in a small town, why wouldn't they know them? Juan immediately spilled his venom of the three, that in school, they were always giving him shit, but were always careful not to go too far because of the school's intolerance of racism and diversity. But, later they continued, long after school, threatening him. More than once, calling him a "wetback from Mexico." He also said, that he and Shara were friends, but that he hadn't talked to her in a few years, but he knows where she lives.

So, Mark told Billy, that we would hopefully have Juan somehow talk to her. He had to see if there was any kind of spark on her end, like he's feeling on his. Probably not, he thought, and Billy was probably right, that she was partying and half drunk.

Juan was more than eager to do anything that would get back at the hated Red, Roland, and Vern.

Meanwhile, in the next few weeks, Tess and Rick were quite happy how the weekends were bearing fruit, as the house and the two barns were rapidly being repaired.

Tess commented, "We should open the Port Wine to have a toast for our success." Without saying a word, Rick went to the small liquor cabinet and said, "Chilled or not?" Tess smiled, walking over, when she suddenly grabbed his genetalia saying, "Baby, I want it chilled. But, I want your hanging fruit red hot," as she pulled down his pants.

Rick was beside himself as he collapsed on the bed, shedding the rest of his clothes, and methodically removing her skirt, blouse, bra, and panties; then he straddled her.

She grabbed his, what seemed like a silo ready for blast off, then said, "Honey, you might think I'm crazy, but your cock seems to get longer and wider as you get older. Can that be true?"

Then she moved down, taking as much as she could, into her throat.

Rick couldn't stop biting on his lower lip, finally pulling it out, "Hold on Honey, let's play around like when we were kids. I want to lick every part of you, from your freckles to your toes.

"Oh, Ricky." Tess exclaimed, "I love you so much."

Then, Rick stood up and Tess admired his muscular body. One again, she grabbed his throbbing manhood as they locked lips, then looking in his eyes, she knew what he wanted to do.

"Oh honey, we haven't done that for a long, long, time."

"I know." Came Rick's response.

Although Tess was forty-two, she always kept in shape. Sex was never an issue, but now, Rick wanted to Flatarm her!

Tess kind of backed up. "Honey, I had a real flat stomach when I was in my twenties and thirties, but now I am over forty."

Rick dropped to his knees, checking out her feet. "My, your feet are the same."

Then he walked his lips, up both toned legs; "And honey, your legs are both the same." He then caressed her around her vagina, then entered her with his tongue.

Tess was moaning in exhilarating bursts of feel good pings, that were exploding deep inside of her.

Then, Rick stood up. Kissing her breasts, Tess knew what was next, as Rick turned her around. "Babe." He was overwhelmed with her beautiful buttocks, "Now, I'm going to flatarm you."

Tess was feeling like little love arrows were weaving in every part of her body. Her genitalia felt like it was on fire, as Rick reached between her legs and with the crook of his elbow, it went right into the recesses of her vagina putting the flat of his hand on her flat stomach. His elbow was in like a 45 position, then twisting, squeezing, and moving sideways and across, the rubbing was over taking her; causing a fire storm of a volcano ready to erupt. But, she wouldn't erupt yet!

She screamed, "Rick, Rick! Do it faster and press harder."

Rick himself, almost ready to climax, just rubbing her, listening to her cry out in raw, wild, gibberish. Finally, Rick heard her holler, then felt the wetness on his arm. Tess turned, grabbing and squeezing his cock, that was ready to punch a hole through the wall. Then she dropped to her knees and mad sucked him, that in less than a minute, he unloads as he pushed her face away as a flying wad flew on the edge of the bed.

With that, they both just cracked up laughter. Tess saying, "I wasn't sure we could pleasure like that again. I guess my genes are still open for your extraordinary love making." Then she went to the window, as Rick wrapped his arms around her; "Sometimes, I wish we lived eons ago, wearing a few animal skins. Then I could take in your beautiful body twenty-four seven."

"Rick, baby," she turned around, "Somehow, I don't think back then, men knew how to flatarm a woman like you do. You know, I never asked you where you learned that from."

Rick rubbing her perky breasts, said, "An army buddy told me he would flatarm his girlfriend. I just remember you standing in our honeymoon suite, and when you turned around, I had to do it."

Tess smiled, "Yes, I remember it well. Come on now, my flatarm extraordinaire, let's go down stairs. I've got to make supper for the gang."

Chapter 6

The next day, a Monday, the twins were plugging in their equipment. Juan and Benny drove up in Juan's Ram pickup, ready for a day's work. It was just the four of them now as Rick had to get back to Park City to his salesman job. Juan, at once told Mark how he was in a food mart last night when he ran into Shara and her mother. Mark's eyes lit up waiting for him to tell him more. Juan in his Spanish accent told him that he quickly came to the point about him as they were getting ready to leave, and that in his few minutes, told her of your affection for her. She looked totally surprised and didn't know what to say.

Juan then said, "Are you still with Roland?"

She said, "Now and then." She started to leave with her mother.

"I thought that was the end of it, when she suddenly stopped, as her mother got in the car, and she said she has her own hair salon now, and to give this card to you." With that, he gave him the card to read. It said "Shara's Beauty Salon;" cuts, nails, manicures, and much more ... 8

Kenworth Ave, Rockville, MA, it listed the shop phone number and an email.

Mark was processing the whole thing, and said "Billy, she must want me to call her." Billy wasn't too impressed, "Look brother, you heard what Juan said. Roland is still in the picture." However, Mark wasn't hearing it, then was trying to map out the best time call her. He knew she would always be busy, so could she really talk to him? Knowing if she did pick up the phone, he would have to get his words right. Maybe she wants him to stop by, or does she? Finally, he opted to take a chance and call her. So around three, he alighted the roof, and called the salon. The person who answered sounded like a young girl. Asking for Shara, the girl said, "Who shall I ask is calling?"

"Mark Martin," ten long seconds then Shara came to the phone. "Hi, Mark. How are you?"

"I'm fine Shara, but you have been on my mind lately."

Shara hesitated a few seconds, then responded. "Yes, we did have a good time at Jimmy's Bar, and I apologize for how the boys roughed you and your brother up." "Well yeah, but you saved us from getting our heads bashed in." She didn't say anything.

Clenching his teeth, he had to ask, "Are you still with Roland?" She responded, "Well, yes and no."

"Well," Mark followed up, "I guess maybe I shouldn't have called."

"No, No." Shara responded, "I'm glad you did. Say, can you meet Harry's Donuts on Route 42 over on Hillberg, tomorrow night; say at seven?" Mark quickly said, "Okay, I know where it is." "Good," Shara concluded; "I'll see you then."

Mark put down the cell, and an aura of golden thoughts swept throughout his mind. When he told Billy, he wasn't too keen on the idea. Reminding him of the trap that Shara was part of.

"I know," was Mark's quiet reply, "Don't worry, I'll watch myself."

Finally, Tuesday night arrived and Mark thought, does she even have a car? Carefully checking the area for the likes of Red, Roland, and Vern, he pulled in, driving Billy's Camaro. Walking in, there was only a few people, but no Shara. Sitting by the window, a half hour had passed, and Mark was wondering if he had been gamed. Then, a Buick Regal pulled up with Shara behind the wheel. His heart racing, seeing her in a yellow summer dress, that highlighted an all-over sexy look. While she was walking in, Mark asked, "Your car?" "No, it's my mom's. But, I have been thinking of getting my own." Mark asked, "How do you like your coffee?"

"Oh, just cream, one sugar."

Then she sat at the table as Mark got the coffee. Thinking to himself, Oh my God, what a beautiful woman. Am I dreaming this? Shara smiling, then kind of giggled. Mark looked puzzled.

"Oh, I was just thinking how we were really partying it up at Jimmy's Bar."

Mark thought, Oh no, she's going to say because we were drunk she was all over me. "Ya, Shara. It was a great time. I hope I won't sound too corny, but to me, I was dancing with a beautiful, stunning, woman."

Looking into her eyes in sincerity, she seemed surprised at that comment, and kind of slapped his shoulder.

"Oh Mark, nobody has ever said that about me before." Mark said, "Not even Roland?"

Shara's black eyes studied him, finally, she conveyed, "Mark, when my mom and myself came to America, we at first lived in the Bronx part of New York. But, it was so depressing, that for over two years, we wanted to move to Providence, Rhode Island, where my mom has a cousin. Finally, it happened, my mom got a job at Walmart, but still, we longed for the country. Although, my mom couldn't speak much English. I learned it in Peru and helped her. Some months later, we saw an ad for a rental in Rockville, and she went to work at the Walmart in Park City. However, after five months, she fell at home and couldn't work anymore. In school, my junior year, I met Roland, he said he would fix it up so that we wouldn't have to worry about rent; if I would go out with him. It was kind of a blackmail, but I knew, for the sake of my mother, whom

I didn't want to have to pack up, yet again, she's too frail as it was; I agreed. So, I have been going out with him ever since. Although, I've been trying to break off, a little at a time."

Mark followed up, "A little at a time?"

"Mark, I know it sounds kind of crazy, but Roland has his good points." He cut her off, "Gee, you could have fooled me."

"Yes, I know. When he's with Vern and Red, he has an evil side. Especially Red."

"So," Mark had to ask, "Does that mean I am not really in the picture?" "Oh, no!" Shara seemed truthful. "I want you in my life. I really mean it."

Mark's euphoria went from near the bottom of the elevator to near the top. Then Shara continued, "The only thing Mark, I am afraid I would put you in danger. Roland would get his two friends and would be looking for you and our brother too."

Mark grabbed her hand, "If you want me in your life, I am going to be in your life; and I wouldn't care if a hundred Roland's were gunning for me."

Shara then embraced him in a hug. "Oh, Mark, you're so nice. Different than anybody I've ever met. They all think they can get me under the sheets."

He thought for a moment then said, "Shara, the real issue is not about my safety, it's about yours."

"Don't worry, Roland wouldn't hurt me, he's in love with me."

Mark wasn't that sure, "Shara, remember him and his friends were going to cave in my and Billy's heads with a golf club? I wouldn't trust him."

So, after agreeing to rendezvous at Harry's in 3 days, they both left for their homes.

Chapter 7

That night, Tess informed the twins, that she would be joining their father in Park City for a couple of weeks to take care of some business. She told them there's frozen dinners in the freezer, while she's gone. Then she pointed out, "You boys behave yourselves, plus your sister and Carson are coming over for the weekend."

Billy remarked, "Carson is as useless as tits on a bull."

"Billy be nice now, we all know he's not a carpenter, but, he helps out." Then she smiled, "So boys, you never told me about those three young women that hauled you away one evening. What happened? No dates?"

Mark replied, "No, Ma. They turned out to be duds."

"Well," Tess replied, "Whatever that means. I'm not going to touch that. So, chow up guys, there's plenty of grub in the freezer. Just don't forget to take it out ahead of time. You both have our cell numbers, and your father has left some cash for the workers. You both know how much they get. You pay them by the day."

Mark got up, bringing his dish to the sink, "Don't worry Mom, we know all that."

Three days passed, and Mark was in Billy's Camaro, going to Harry's to meet Shara once again. Pulling up, he saw the green Buick

Regal was already there. His heart jumped as he walked in, seeing her in a pair of pink shorts and a halter top.

Shara smiled, "Hi, Mark. Good to see you again, and I got you an iced coffee that you like."

"Please Shara, I don't want you buying me things. I know money is tight with you andyour mother."

"Don't worry about it, it's not that bad since I opened the salon." So, Mark tried to get in her mind without bringing up Roland.

"You work all the time? Do you ever have any time off in the day?"

Shara took a sip, "Not too much Mark, but I have been thinking about you often." A big smile crossed his face. I think about you too."

Shara instructed him to come around the table to sit next to her. "I don't bite you know."

Mark was captivated in emotion as he sat close to her. Then she suggested, "Say, why don't we grab our brews, and sit in Billy's Camaro, I always loved these fast cars."

"Ya," Mark quipped, "My brother recently put in a 396, replacing the original that was getting tired."

Shara squinted her eyes, "396, does that mean the motor?" "Yes." Mark kind of chuckled.

Sitting in the car, they were further apart than in the coffee shop. Then Shara said, "Mark, there's a side road about a mile down on the right. What do you say we drive there?"

Mark put the car in drive, and they quickly drove down the dirt road. Mark deliberately going in crawl, said "Billy will kill me if I get his "baby" all dirty."

"Don't worry, there's a small pond up ahead, pull up next to it."

With that, as the bright moon shone across the water, he pulled over. "It looks like a nice area." Mark a little stargazed managed to say.

Shara then suggested that they should get in the back, because of the console. However, the back seat wasn't especially roomy, as he wanted so much to put his arms around her. Shara could see that he was kind of shy and embraced him. Mark now, was more willing to show his emotions. But, he remembered what she said about guys trying to get her underneath the sheets, but when Shara kissed him, he felt more like a teenager than twenty-four.

"Relax Mark, you seem to be uptight."

"Sorry Shara. I just always get nervous at first." "There's no need to be," she smiled.

Her second kiss was like a locked door that was opened, and Mark knew he was now in her willing arms. He planted a long, sensual, soft kiss, when Shara said, "That's more like it. I'm glad you're not so stiff."

Of course, that wasn't entirely right, for between his legs, his best friend was pushing against his jeans. Mark tried to keep her from finding that out, as he kind of got sideways, but he knew, that she felt him as they were squirming around. Then, he tried to slow down, to relax his manhood tearing out his underwear.

Shara smiled, "Mark, you're so handsome."

Of course, that didn't help as his cock again went to the firing mode. Then Mark suggested that they get out, to looks across the moonlight pond.

"Okay." Shara agreed.

Then, they stood hand in hand in front of the Camaro. She again embraced him, and Mark knew, that he was under her whim; that she oversaw his emotions. "You are a gorgeous chick," he managed to get the words out. Again, she gave that smile, that melted him.

"Oh Mark, I am really fond of you. Do you think you can get away from the farm next Monday to go to the mall with me in Park City?"

"Yes, I can. As long as my brother lets me use his car." "Well," Shara paused, "Never mind that, I'll pick you up."

Mark thought, then said, "I don't like to bring up the "dark side," but what about Roland?"

"Fuck Roland." The outburst completely took him by surprise. "He doesn't own me." Mark thought he has said enough. "What time Monday?"

"Around noon would be good," she reflected as they headed back to drop her to get her car.

He was feeling like a million dollars, that he soon would be spending the afternoon with her. Of course, after telling Billy about his plans, Billy was worrying about Roland finding out;and God knows what he would do.

That weekend, Cassie and Carson came over again. When Carson saw Mark going into one of the barns, he followed him.

"Hey Mark. Looks like you and the rest have almost finished the repairs."

"Yeah," Mark said, "It went rather smoothly." Then he thought, no thanks to you dick weed.

"Say, Billy told us about your obsession with a Spanish girl." "Yeah, so what about it?"

"Nothing really. Except, he says she has a piece of shit boyfriend." "Don't worry Carson, I'll deal with my own affairs."

Carson just turned around and went back to the house.

Later, that afternoon, Billy said he was going to the store to buy some smokes. After chowing and enjoying one of Cassie's homemade chicken pies.

Mark questioned, "Where's Billy?"

Cassie shrugged her shoulder saying, "I told him supper was at 6."

After a couple more hours went by, Mark started to worry. When Carson suggested, "Why don't we jump in the Lexus and take a ride to the store."

Mark was concerned, "I worry that 69' Camaro could be a magnet for someone to try and steal it, then they went to the Rockville Variety. The only store on this side of town."

Mark told the clerk that a young guy driving a red Camaro was supposed to be going here earlier.

"Did he come in and buy smokes?"

"Well, ya," the clerk hesitated, "In fact, he looks like you."

"Bulls-eye, my friend. He's my twin."

The clerk said, "He left right away, probably around 3 o'clock, when I was starting my shift."

Back in the car, Mark related what the clerk said, saying, "Let's go back to the house to see if he called the land line. There's nothing on my cell."

Carson pointed out, that "Cassie would call us if that was the case." "Yeah, that's true. I wonder where he went?"

At the house, Mark knew it was time to tell his sister and Carson about the run-in with Roland and his friends. Cassie, alarmed by the disclosure, thought they should call their parents. "Not yet, Sis. Give Billy until morning. Maybe he got hooked up with some broad. You know Billy isn't bashful."

The next morning came with no sight of Billy. Cassie was distraught.

"That classic car of his could have been carjacked. Or, maybe he ran into those "roughen" s."

"Come on Mark," Carson nodded to his car, "Let's ride around and see if we can find the Camaro."

Meanwhile, in Park City, Tess hooked up with her best friend Fay for an afternoon of shopping, then out to dinner before Rick and her headed back to Rockville.

"So," Fay was eager to hear about the farmhouse, "How goes the renovations?"

"Actually, quite good," Tess responded. "Rick hired a couple of townies, and of course the twins are carpenters. Cassie and Carson help out too."

Then, more mundane conversation, Tess had to ask, "Fay, you and I are about the same age … Do you still have the same drive, when it comes to sex?"

Fay, an attractive brunette, who has known Tess since the fifth grade laughed, "Well, now and then, but I think for the most part Ken initiates our romps."

Tess didn't say anything, and Fay said, "Honey, you are having a problem with Rick?" "No, no! Not at all. In fact, the other night, we really got into it."

"Yeah?" Fay came back. "Hot, sizzling sex?"

Tess had a sensual grin, "Oh, it was. Fay, I was flatarmed."

"What does that mean?"

"It's something Rick does to me but hasn't done it in a long time."

"Come on darling, what in the devil are you talking about?"

"Well," Tess continued, "I suppose couples do it, but I doubt they call it being flat- armed."

Fay was now beyond curious, "What's being flatarmed mean?"

Tess smiled. "Fay, when I'm standing with nothing on, with my back to him. He reaches between my legs, with the flat of his arm between the recesses of my vagina, then putting the flat of his hand on my stomach, he moves the crook of his arm into me. Rubbing, pressing, moving up and down, sideways; causing a friction that's hard to describe. Maybe I should say it goes a lot longer than the usual flash point of feeling, that the climax coming is driving you crazy. Maybe it's just me, but it's like being on a roller coaster. The tingles of riding to the top, then at every high point, I just lose it in exhilarating bursts. In fact, I was so insatiably drained, that I sucked his cock with such a tenacity, that his wad went flying onto the side of the bed."

Fay was beyond shocked, "It really sounds beyond spectacular."

"Oh Fay, the climax was something every woman should experience. You and Ken should try it."

But before she could answer, the cell rang, it was Cassie.

"Mom," she cried out, "Billy's missing."

With that, Rick and Tess headed for Rockville.

When they arrived later that night, Billy's Camaro was in the driveway. Rushing out to meet them, was Mark, Cassie, and Carson.

"What happened?" Rick blared out.

Cassie quickly told them, that only an hour ago Billy drove in, but he wasn't drunk, but it was like he was on drugs. He was slurring, mumbling gibberish, completely out of it. Then, Mark said, "That's not like him, he always stayed away from drugs."

They all went up to the bedroom to check on him, but, he wouldn't cooperate. Just telling them he needed to sleep.

Tess said, "He sounds like he's on something."

Cassie removed his shoes, saying, "Maybe we should call a doctor." Rick followed up, "They would want to see him."

Billy looked over slurring, "I'm good, need rest. Leave me alone."

"Come on everybody," Rick nodded, "Let him sleep it off."

The next morning, as the crew was around the breakfast table, Mark remarked, "I checked his car, no problem there."

Coming down the stairs, was bug eyed Billy; shirtless and not solid on his feet. Rick said, "Are you okay son?"

Billy nodded that he was fine. Tess told him to put on a shirt. As Billy turned to get it, Cassie dropped her jaw.

"Look at his back!"

Billy hearing her, "What about my back?"

Everyone gathered around him. Someone told him, that his back looked like tiny tattoos of hex symbols.

Carson thought they looked like panograms. "And you have scratches on your middle area," Carson added.

Finally, he went through how after he got smokes, he felt in the mood for a smoothie. He drove to Park City, when he ran into Cindy Lou. Then, one thing led to another, and they went to a motel that she paid for.

"Cindy Lou? The red head from the three moron boyfriends?"

"Yeah," Billy, kind of embarrassed, nodded. "I spent the night with her."

Mark grinned, "Well, it looks like you did. Looking at the scratches on your back." Tess was rightly concerned, "Son, how did you get these tattoos?"

Billy was extremely distraught. "I don't know Mom. I thought my back was smarting from her nails. Everything seemed to be a blur."

Rick followed up, "When you're feeling better, I think we should take you to the clinic." "No!" Billy strongly discounted. "I'm fine!"

Mark went to the computer to check on the symbols, "Holy shit," he half yelled,

"Although they're small, one is a pentagram goat, patch, a devil symbol, and the other is called a Restyle Lucifer signal occult; another devil symbol."

"Those three bitches must have set me up," Billy quickly said. "Hold on brother," Mark was combative, "Shara is no bitch!"

Before he could continue, Rick interjected. "You guys aren't telling us everything."

Finally, Mark went through how they were threatened with getting their heads bashed in and how Shara saved their asses.

Rick voiced, "You mean, Mark, you're taking one of them out?"

"That I am, and for a while now. In fact, I think I'm in love with her." "What?" Tess was alarmed. "Mark, do you really know much about her?"

Cassie was on the same line, "This devil stuff might include you too. May have been played by all three girls. … like a devils web."

"Oh Cassie, you always were reading about cult stuff."

Rick, then looking out the window, thought it would be wise to find out if there's any history of any kind of devil worshiping in Rockville.

Billy laughed, "I just think Cindy Lou marked me on Red's orders to scare me."

"No," Rick was adamant, "They didn't go to all that trouble to tattoo you. Having doped you up, there's a real sinister event going on in this town."

After breakfast, Rick and Tess decided to try and get an audience with the Chief of Police, to see what they could learn.

Juan and Benny arrived for the last few days of work. Mark questioned them about a cult, but they had no idea. However, it was Shara he really wanted to talk to, so he decided to drive to the salon. Borrowing C arson's Lexus, he came in sight of the beauty parlor. Catching his eye, was Roland, coming out the front door, and jumping into the Ford F150 that apparently belonged to Red. An unfamiliar chill over took him. Shara told him she was pretty much done with Roland. So, he waited about an hour to see if she mentioned Roland. Later, driving in, parking beside her mother's Buick, he went inside. Shara was cutting a customer's hair, when she looked; then excusing herself, she walked over.

"Mark, what a surprise. Something up?"

"I know this is a bad time, but I need to talk to you about something. Can you get away for about ten minutes?"

"Of course, let me finish this cut. You sit down, I won't be long."

About twenty minutes or so, and she motioned him to go by her car. "What's up Hon?"

Mark surprised, "Hey, that's the first time you've called me Hon." "Hey," she responded smiling, "Just maybe I like you."

Then, he told her about what has unfolded with Billy.

Shara looked astute, "My God," she explained, "Devil symbols? I never heard of anything in Rockville about witch craft, or anything that ever came close, and Cindy Lou, as long as I've known her, she never talked about that stuff."

"What about Roland, your boyfriend?"

"Mark, he's not my boyfriend anymore, and guess what you are? In fact, I haven't seen him in days."

That last comment sent a bevy of red flags that she was lying. Mark, then tried to process what her intent with him really was. Maybe she's part of this devil witch craft shit. Maybe she at least knows about it. They say some people in South American countries still practice that kind of stuff.

Shara looked disappointed, "I guess you won't be going to the mall tomorrow?"

Mark gulped, he had to make a quick decision. Seeing him hesitate, she voiced, "It's okay Mark. With all that is going on …"

"No, I'm going. I need some R & R."

"Good," Shara seemed ecstatic, "I'll pick you up at noon."

In the meantime, Rick and Tess came away, after meeting Chief Dan Porter of the Rockville P.D. But, he was quick to say, there has been nothing on record or anything of that kind. When Mark returned Carson's silver Lexus back, he told him that in the coming week, he was borrowing money off his father to buy a vehicle from one of his father's friends.

That night, as the twin decided to hit the hay, Mark focused on the symbols. "What are you going to do about those tattoos?"

Billy answered, "I'm going to have them removed."

Mark looked into his brother's face, "I hope to hell, you don't team with that Cindy Lou again. Isn't she that Vern's girlfriend?"

"Yeah, no shit. That Vern may be the quiet one, but Cindy Lou says he's on probation for assault and battery with intent to maim. I know I shouldn't have gone to the motel with her, but you know the old saying … A stiff prick has no conscience."

"Yeah, and you got scarred up."

Mark then walked over to the window, "You know, ever since this crap started; I have been on the computer googling up the European Witch Trials. Germany, for one, was extremely brutal. If one neighbor had a beef with another, they would tell the authorities that they were using black magic; and if a few friends of the accuser went along with it, the person was arrested, searched, then shaved; looking for the devil's mark. In those days, a devil mark could have been a mole, skin tag, blemish; anything really. Then the witch finders would say the devil was sucking them. The next step was torture that never stopped, until they confessed. They usually just confessed to stop the brutal pain, then blamed others for being witches; and they were completely innocent. Just goes on and on."

"Shit. Nice people." Billy voiced. "But, this is the twenty-first century, not the dark ages."

"It doesn't matter brother, there's been sporadic outbursts of witch craft, even in Black Masses; for centuries, including the United States."

"So, what you're saying Mark, is that this is for real?" It just doesn't make sense, that a small town like Rockville, and nobody knows anything."

The next day, Shara picked up Mark for their trip to the mall in Park City. Although the Roland episode put a sour taste in Mark's mouth, it didn't change the euphoria of being with her. As they headed for the city, Billy was getting restless. Knowing that the repairs were for the most part finished, when out of the blue, he got a text from Cindy Lou; wanting to meet up at Harry's Donuts. Although everyone warned him to stay away from her, he just couldn't, knowing that she must know something about the tattoos. Before he left, he strapped a good-sized hunting knife around his waist.

Before he pulled into the parking lot, he canvased the area for the likes of Vern, Red, and Roland. Finally parking next to the blue Camry, he was thinking how she marked his back, or, someone did. Walking in, she had a big smile, "Hello Billy, I didn't think you would show."

In a harsh voice, Billy replied, "Why? Because you doped me up and drew devil symbols on my back?"

She pointed out, "We're here to talk. I got two coffees, the owner doesn't like when people come in to shoot the breeze and not buy anything."

"Let's cut out the small talk, let's hear it. Was I not man enough for you? You had to put tattoos on my back?"

"Don't be ridiculous. I didn't do that. The Order did."

"What "Order?"" Billy came down hard. "Maybe I should go to the cops." "Relax Billy, please sit down and I'll explain everything." Billy looked around glad that there were several customers around. He kept his eyes peeled to the window for the likes of Vern.

"The Order is a society that meets to come together for the purpose to rethink one's self on many aspects of the world, as we know it."

"What are you talking about?" Billy was getting hot under the collar. "Is it devil shit?" "Calm down Billy, I know you're a fun guy. You'll love what the society offers. Getting high, booze or drugs, or both. Sex. Even which includes orgies. Unlimited access to money. Instead of going through the drudgery of occasional sex, when your partner wants it."

"It sounds weird," Billy responded, "First of all, I don't do drugs except for pot. I love my liquor." Then he asked, "What about the devil's symbols on my back?"

"What religion are you Billy?" "Baptist!"

She was surprised, "I would have thought in these parts you would've been Catholic or Protestant."

"Yeah, well my father met my mother while he was in the Army. Stationed in Nebraska, she is a Baptist."

Cindy Lou then elaborated, "Once you come to the meeting you'll see other things to enjoy, and all of the inner workings that control the thought, are of course, a higher force."

He was torn to listen, just get up and leave, or take in the bullshit. But he had to find out who marked him.

"Billy," Cindy Lou looked into his eyes, "Vern may be my boyfriend for now, but, the society order allows us to wander at will. I must make a confession. Before the motel, when we drove you guys to our so-called boyfriends, we were told by the society to see if you could be potential members of our secret organization. You will soon discover the real central authority, who really controls us. To live life, away from the usual norms, not a Jayo Christian, do everything right, Miss Goody Two Shoes, and such. You will say it's a party all the time."

"So, what are in this society?"

"I, along with Karen and Shara, are the head witch disciples to a larger group."

But, before Billy could react, she pointed out; "We are disciples to the altar of the occult, who are no evil witches, but witches who adore the society and all its power. I want you, my handsome lover, to join our cause."

Billy shook his head, "Sorry Cindy Lou, I don't think I want to."

Cindy sipped her coffee, "Billy, there is however a caveat for refusal."

"What's that mean?"

"Billy, since you have already been marked, that if you refuse it; it could mean you'll be harmed."

"You're scaring me Cindy. It's a devil cult, and I can't believe Shara is in this too."

"Billy," Cindy Lou clutched his hand, "I never wanted you to be marked, but you're going to have to deal with it. Besides, I was playing you along at first. In fact, I couldn't stand you and probably would have laughed if Red beat the fuck out of you, but now, I see just a fun- loving 24-year-old, that wants to explore the tantalizing gifts, that only the society can bring."

"Cindy Lou, we only spent one night together, you really don't know anything about me."

me?"

"I know enough," was her answer, "Next Friday night is our next meeting, will you join Billy was afraid to go and afraid not to go.

"I know," Cindy came across, "There is a lot of unknown, but you're going to have to trust me. Come on handsome guy, let's blow this place. Follow me to my apartment."

Billy, still uptight and thinking that might not be a good idea, until she said, "I want to play house with Billy Man."

So, against his better judgement, he followed her to her digs.

Chapter 8

Later that night, Shara pulled in the driveway of the old farmhouse "Hey Mark, I had a fantastic time. How about you?"

Mark moved over closer to her and said, "You're a beautiful woman Shara." Then he planted a long, lip lock, as Shara responded by clutching his genitals. "Wow," Mark smiled, "I didn't expect that."

Shara grinned, "So when will I see you again?" "Not fast enough." "Well, call me at the salon, okay?" "Will do Shara."

Then he went to the house and noticed Billy's Camaro was gone. His cell rang, it was his father's friend Jessie Redding. He said that he's driving to the farm with the 06' Ford Edge that Mark had bought. Soon, Mark had his own wheels. A silver Ford Edge. Short mileage, good condition, and his father had it registered and insured, and he only had to sign a few papers. But, of course, he had to find some carpentry work; probably in Park City, to pay for it.

Later that night, Rick and Tess, along with Cassie and Carson arrived from going out to dinner. Everybody was alarmed that Billy once again never came home.

The next morning, Cassie and Carson had to get back to their jobs in Park City.

When leaving, Cassie said, "Make sure you call us when he comes home. That brother of mine is stressing me out."

Carson laughed, "Probably just sowing his oats."

"Not funny Carson. Was he sowing his oats when he got the devil symbols on his back?" That same morning, Cindy Lou walked out with Billy to his car smiling. "So, stud master, will I see you Friday night?"

Billy knew that he must take a chance to find out what really is going on and would have to trust her.

"Okay, I'll go."

"Good, I'm glad. I'll pick you up at your house. About 6:00pm."

Cindy Lou grabbed his shoulder as he got into the Camaro and then she began, "Don't say word about what we talked about to your family, and especially your twin. If the society finds out, I might be harshly disciplined."

Billy, now behind the wheel hesitated, "I thought the society was all good order of what's missing in our lives?"

"It is," Cindy Lou replied, "But, like many secret organizations, it must stay secret."

Billy put his fingers to his lips, "My lips are sealed."

Cindy Lou reached over, planting a kiss, then responded with, "I love your car. When can I drive it?"

"Soon." Billy smiled.

He took off and headed for the farm.

Rick was repairing a small utility building when the sun caught the gleaming chrome bumper as Billy pulled in. His mother was inside baking some chocolate chip cookies, when Billy walked in.

"Hi Mom. These cookies smell good."

"As soon as they cool off, help yourself." Tess responded. Rick, then joined them.

"Hi, Dad. I see you're working on the utility shed."

"Yeah," Rick said, "We can use it for storage." Then Billy asked, "Where's brother Mark?"

"Oh, he bought Jessie Redding's SUV. Probably out driving around."

"Hey, that's awesome. Now, I don't have to worry about him getting my baby all dirty." "Well," Tess looked out the window, "We've had great weather lately, but looking at the sky, I think it's about to change."

That night, as a semi tropical rain belted the area, Mark decided to turn in, when Billy had the same idea.

"So, Mark, this storm will be a real test of our carpenter skills."

"Yeah brother. We would be in deep shit right now if that roof leaked. So, how was your latest romp with Cindy Lou?"

"Oh, she's one hot broad. She took care of ole' Billy."

"Yeah?" Mark laughed. "How many more devil symbols on your body?" Billy now nude, got into bed, "The two you seen from before."

"Then, maybe I should ask a stupid question. Did you find out who the mysterious tattoo artist was? Or was its Cindy Lou?"

"No Mark, it wasn't Cindy Lou. Now let the questions lie. I'm beat! Sometimes, massive foreplay and humping away, can drive a man beyond tired."

All Mark said was, "I hope the hell you know what you're doing."

Chapter 9

The next day, a Saturday, Mark took his parents to the diner called John Smalley's in Rockville. Rick and Tess had visited it before, for their great burgers and onion rings. Billy decided not to go, to wash and wax the Camaro SS, when his cell rang.

"Hi, my love, it's me Cindy Lou. Just wanted to relay that I told the society about you, and they can't wait to meet you Friday night."

"Okay," Billy was quick to reply, "Cindy, I am really doing it because of you." "Okay Babe. Keep in touch."

A few minutes after the call, he got to thinking. Maybe he should tell Mark about what's going on. But, then again could Cindy Lou be harmed? And yet again, was he being played big time by her?

After a while, the car was super clean and shining, and though, as much as he and Mark jostle each other sometimes to see who could stick the needle in the deepest, so to speak; If he ever revealed Shara is a disciple, to weird devil organization, it would put poor brother on his head. There were so many questions, very few answers, so he had to keep mum and see exactly what this "society" was.

Finally, Friday rolled around, when Mark noticed Billy put on some clean duds. "A date, my good brother?"

"That's right."

Mark just shook his head, knowing it's probably with Cindy Lou. Soon, Cindy Lou picked him up and they headed for the meeting with the "society". Billy noted, that they were taking a lot of dirt roads, when he said, "Hey Cindy, this place must really be in the boondocks."

After more twisting and turning, Cindy Lou pointed out, that they would be stopped at the Anti Heaver Gate. Billy flinched, but had to act that he was ready for whatever they threw at him; hiding an inert fear. A small building, then came into focus. It was surrounded by an iron gate. Two burly men wearing black type pullover shirts and hoods, with blazing flames on the front approached them as Cindy Lou parked the car.

"Now, don't be alarmed Billy. It's all controlled by the society." The man escorted them to the gate.

Then Cindy Lou said, "This is Billy Martin. I think he will be a good asset to the organization."

One of the men told Billy to come with him. Billy saw that Cindy Lou suddenly vanished. The man led him into a small room, as Billy noted the outline of a gun holster was pushing back his shirt, and then knew he was packing a gun. He told him to put on an oversized shirt; one with pentagrams, like the tattoos on his back. Without saying a word, Billy was blindfolded and frozen in fear.

"No need to worry." The man sounded like an elderly person, and then he led him down a winding path.

Then, maybe after ten minutes or so, after he had been led over a staircase, and going what it seemed by the temperatures, deeper into the ground. Then he heard laughing and people talking. The blindfold was removed, and the first thing he saw, was a wide-open room, with people gambling. There were crap tables, black jack, slot machines, and other things, that one would find in Lams Vegas. The air, heavy with marijuana and other burning substances. Then the man led him through a psychedelic door. In a side room, he heard what sounded like people having sex. A partly opened door, confirmed it, as naked bodies were everywhere. Then, in another room, people doing drugs, including smoking from a bong. Up ahead, was an auditorium, with people taking seats. The walls were covered with weird signs, and hex circles, and a huge portrait of Satan.

A robed bifocal man confronted him, saying, "You, my friend, have been chosen to be a member of the Society. Now, what you've seen is not all we're about, although, sex and drugs, are paramount to young people today. But, our underlying message, is that we are the embodiment of the Anti-Christ Movement. We live life on the edge, usually, if we want something bad enough we will steal it. We don't follow the rules of what's right and wrong. We believe Christ is mostly a myth. Our allegiance is to Satan, who controls a part of each and everybody; and, if you believe in Christ, he is losing the battle for our souls. Billy, we believe life is short and final, that we must fulfill our ambitions while we are going through the trials of life. Now, we have several prominent benefactors, who support our cause with hard cash; and members pay a token to the coffers, to keep generators, food, recreational drugs, beer and liquor, and life's mundane things. But, my young man, we must be able to trust you. So, what do you think?"

"I am so confused. I don't know what to think. Why was I tattooed? I have to know." "Well," the man kind of sneered, "A fair question. From our information on you, your profile was of an adventurous personality. Trying anything that would fit very nicely in the realm of the society."

Then he motioned a small man over, wearing the same type of robe; wearing thick glasses. He instructed him by saying, "Jerome, take our young friend to taste the forbidden fruit." Jerome pointed to a small enclave, where three scantily clad young woman were sitting around a table, that was covered in tapestry of a sinister time, called "The Burning Times." Billy stood there, not sure what to do, when another woman joined them, and said, "Hello Billy. Remember me? I am Karen."

Of course, she was covered in a black robe, with different with craft symbols. Then, Billy remembered that Cindy Lou had said that her, Karen, and Shara were disciples.

Then, she said "Welcome to the society." Then she motioned to the three young women, and told them, in short shifts, to get food and drink for their "new friend."

They quickly sat Billy down, and he was given everything, from cuts of meats, to grapes, black berries and pomegranates.

Karen said, "Billy, show the girls the symbols on your back." Billy hesitated.

"Take off your shirt Billy. Don't be bashful. Besides, before long, you will have everything off."

He slipped his shirt off, and the girls seemed to be in a trance. They ogled his tattoos, touching; then quickly retreated to their seats in the controlled order.

Karen walked over, "Well Billy, boy, I am glad Red didn't cave your head in. You will be a great asset to our movement."

Then, one of the girls of Karen's, sign language produced a white line on the table, that Billy knew was probably cocaine.

"No, no," he put his hand up. He wasn't going to be suddenly under a false-minded substance.

"It's okay Billy, you're now part of the order."

Its fringe pleasures supersede only I could, or would" Then Karen walked out of the enclave. The three women surrounded him, pulling his pants and grabbing his genitals. Billy thought, no, this isn't real!

Hours later, he awoke. Knowing that he had done lines of coke. As the girls, were gone;

he knew he had sex with all of them.

Then, the short guy Jerome came in, saying, "Come on Billy. Let me help you to the shower."

Billy groggily asked for a towel.

Jerome smiled, "After the shower." Then, eying his genitals, he remarked, "My, my. Your cock and balls are well equipped to satisfy the trollops."

Billy couldn't wait to get in the shower, as Jerome, accidentally, on purpose, touched his buttocks. After the shower, he was given back his clothes. Then, with Cindy Lou, they went to the entrance.

"Are you okay? How did the girls treat you?"

Billy looked kind of pissed off. "Cindy, you know what happened. It's going to take more than dope and sex to control me."

Cindy Lou didn't answer.

"Come on, I'll drive you home."

Billy then asked, "I saw Karen, where's Shara?"

Cindy Lou got in his face. "Don't be such a fool. You never ask questions about this place, got it?"

Billy recognized his immaturity. "Okay, okay!"

On the way back, Cindy Lou told him, that in two weeks, the society would be having a ceremony honoring the victims of "The Burning Times." He looked at the fiery red head.

"What's the burning times?"

"That is what history calls the European Witch Hunts. It's where thousands of women, and some men, were falsely accused of witchcraft, and burned alive. Satan's demons have ordered it according to the society."

Then, Billy remembered Mark talking about it. "I don't think I follow you. Satan's demons?"

"Well," Cindy Lou, extracting a cigarette from a gold case continued, "Satan has relished the Burning Times, because it kept the witchcraft mania on everybody's mind, and that more relevant. According to the society, he was behind a lot of trials, that caused men and women to burn, that way their souls would be claimed by him and his demons. Then, their souls would be park of the Dark Chasm that is hell. Where he has resurrected their ashes and were made part of the army to defeat Christ."

Billy said, "I don't believe that bullshit. Why would he get their souls and not God?" Cindy Lou surprised him, when she said, "I don't believe it either, but I follow the line;
and bear in mind, the society, is also a bank for its members."
"Bank?"
"Yeah," Cindy Lou continued, "Anyone that's in trouble, has the right to borrow cash, for any legitimate reason. But, I wouldn't recommend it, then they would own you. In fact, that's why I chose to seduce you. For cash, so they could mark up your body."
"Why you bitch!" Billy yelled.
"Relax Billy don't do anything foolish. You're in to stay, and remember, the society knows all about your family. And, believe me, they are vicious. If you ever spill the beans or bring the law down, I'm afraid they would burn the farm house down, with everybody in it."
"And you?" Billy asked. "Would you help them?"
"No, I wouldn't. Would you believe, I was going to Boston University, studying journalism, when I left and got into this stuff?"
Billy felt like a wall was closing around him. Knowing that he was getting to the point, where he was going to be locked in.
"Why did you get into this stuff?" Billy inquired. "It's a long story."
Back in his driveway now, Cindy Lou said, "I'll be in touch. Remember, what happened to you, never happened! Keep mum, especially to your twin." With that, Billy walked into the house.
It was around 6:30 in the morning. Billy noted that his Dad's 350 1 ton was gone. Then Mark came driving down the driveway.
"Hey, look at you; in the o6' Ford Edge," exclaimed Billy, "Finally got your own wheels."
"Yeah, Billy boy," Mark concluded, "Probably feels as good as when you stick it in Cindy Lou."
"Ha, ha. Very funny. You're just pissed because you're not getting anything from Shara. Or has she fixed your problem?"
Bursting into laughter, Mark spewed out, "Very funny, Moron," and he walked away.

Chapter 10

The next day, Billy was on the computer, when he saw that in Park City, there was an old car show a week from Friday.

"Alright," he yelled out, "I have been waiting to take her." Suddenly though, his joy came crashing down, "Shit," he thought; "That's the day of the Burning Times night. Who the hell wants to go to that. I'd rather take Cindy Lou to the show, then spend the night with her. I'm not a fan of multi-sex, and drugs. God knows what you might catch."

By coincidence, Mark called Shara about a date on the same Friday night to go to a movie. Shara told him that she was taking her mother to Providence, Rhode Island to visit her cousin and that she regretted that she couldn't make it. So, that was said and done.

Rick and Tess arrived from a trip to Park City, where Rick purchased a small tractor for the farm. The twins greeted them as they got out; telling them, that the new John Deere tractor should be there in a few weeks.

"Hey," Mark joked, "Green Acres is the place for me."

Billy added, "Did you get one with a four speed on the floor, so we can drag the neighbors?"

Rick smiled, "Not quite Billy. However, I am sure there's plenty of power for the farm." "What are you going to call it?" Mark asked. Rick looked around, "You know, it's so quiet around here; I'm going to call it Peaceful Acres." Then added, "Next year I'm buying some live stock and milk cows. Buckle up guy's before you know it will be a bonafide working farm!

That Friday night, that Billy both dreaded and look forward again to, seeing Cindy Lou who he was dangerously falling for her company; came along, as she picked him up for the Burning Times Rally. Rick, Juan, Mark, and Benny planned to play poker on the farmers porch, as Cindy Lou's Camry would head for the rendezvous with the society.

Billy said, "Cindy, you seem quiet tonight. What's up?" "Oh, nothing, I just hope everything goes well."

"What do you mean?"

"Well," she began, "I heard there was some internal trouble, but I'm not sure." Billy reflected, "No doubt they will blindfold me like before."

"Of course," Cindy was quick to answer, "You're on a probation period. But, whatever happens tonight, keep yourself focused and pretend you like the proceeding."

Billy just blinked his eyes as they moved quickly to the checkpoint, and tried to memorize the way, when Cindy commented, "Oh, I am going to a different maze of roads, and by the way, the society has dummy checkpoints at different places. So, "neophytes" like you couldn't bring down the heat. It's standard procedure. Of course, I am sure you wouldn't, in lieu of what of what I told you about the society's vicious past."

Billy didn't say anything. Soon they were there. He noted four bikers pulling up, packing sexy women in leather, with New York plates. Then, three limos pulled up, where scores of well- dressed men and women alighted. But, the biggest surprise, was what looked like a customized, full sized bus. It arrived sporting New Jersey plates, and young people piled out; almost like they were going to a basketball game or some other sports venue.

Cindy Lou grabbed his hand, "C'mon champ. Just stay cool."

After that, he was then blindfolded, and descended into the vaults of the underground. He was led into what looked like an off-shoot cave. Cindy then went in a different direction. He was told by a society member, to sit in a row in the back. Then, maybe forty-five minutes passed, when a long, large screen on wheels, was pushed to the forefront. Then, suddenly, it was a blazing display of a wall of fire. A man in a tan suit, who was draped over in an open cloak, appeared on the stage for his orientation.

"Friends, Welcome to the Devil's Workshop. I am Pearl Jam," he snickered. "No affiliation with the band of course."

Billy could hear eerie music coming from hidden speakers.

Then, again the man spoke, "Like I said, I am Pearl Jam. Part of the inner circle, where we circumvent history's written account of the Burning Times; with the truth of what it is my friends. Sure, many thousands, were burnt at the stake, supposedly innocent, during the witch trials. In the 15th and 16th centuries, all over Europe, notably Germany, Switzerland, France, Poland, and many more locations. However, only less than one third, were innocent. The rest were agents of Satan, and we have gathered here to commemorate their souls to Satan. Many thousands were doing the Devil's work, when they were arrested, tortured, and burned alive. And now, the Prince of Darkness, controls their soul. Now, to be fair, people have asked me, why do you worship the devil? Well, I'll tell you why. Satan, the fallen angel, in his battle with the one called God, and his messengers, like Christ, Mohammed, Buddha, and all the rest. Was there any time, that wars and killing, were stopped across the bloody chapter of the centuries? The Roman enslavement, the Crusades, and the Ottoman Empire, and the two World Wars. I could go on for hours. Did anything change? No, it didn't. Millions, were enslaved, massacred or reduced to abject poverty. Satan, my friends, people who believe in him, will break the chains of organized religion and crush those who go against him. Here in the society, in the Devil's workshop, we are following his wishes, to take what we want. So, with that; beside me, there are three buckets, with tiny bits of the tortured and burned tongues of the victims of the Burning Times. So, my friends, you will kneel and drink from the cup. But, before that, turn your attention to the Chief Warlock of the Devil's Workshop, Criptin."

"Ah," Criptin smiled, "Pearl Jam has outlined our philosophy and gave you an unvarnished history of the Burning Times."

Criptin, was an older man, was wearing a black winged cloak, ornamented with Satan on his chest.

He then said, "Prepare the ceremony!"

Three men came to the front, wearing those hooded cloaks with flames. Billy knew he was looking at Red, Roland, and Vern. The three then gathered scores of cups, that would be placed in the cauldron, filled with a yellow broth. Billy turned white, looking at what looks like vile waste. Criptin looked, to the probably seventy to eighty people hinged on his very words.

"Once again, you have proven to be loyal to Satan, by attending the Burning Times Rally. As for you new people, let me say, the victims who were burned eons ago, you must realize, that only Satan resurrected their burned souls from their ashes. So, my fellow devil worshipers, come forth while my disciples prepare the broth for your consumption."

Billy looked for a way out, but two stern faced society members were eying him. He knew he had to drink the yellow broth, knowing that if he refused to, or tried to escape, they'd probably have Red, Roland, and Vern really fuck him up. He was sure Vern knew about him going to Cindy Lou's apartment. Was this part of the plan to steal his soul? Then, the three put the gold cups into the broth. Suddenly appearing, was Cindy Lou, Karen, and Shara; when the three so-called boyfriends passed the cups to the so-called disciples, as people got up and knelt in front of the Burning Times display, saying, "In Satan we believe." Then, one by one, they consumed the broth.

Now, the last row was to follow suit. Billy braced himself to drink from the cup. None of the Rockville women acted like they knew him. When Cindy Lou gave the broth to him to drink, the smell and taste almost bowled him over.

When everybody was seated, Criptin exclaimed his joy; that Satan would be pleased and the battle to kill Christ will continue at break neck speed.

"Oh my God," Billy thought. Although he was never much for going to church, but to kill Christ. This is a warped cult, that somehow, someway must be taken down.

Back again, with Cindy Lou in her car, on their trip back to the farm; she didn't say much, until they were a few miles from the long driveway of the farm.

"Well Billy, I now know that you are not going to be convinced that Satan is really the Almighty, and not God."

"That's right Cindy, and on what you told me before, you don't believe this crap either." "Shh, shh," she cautioned him, "They might have planted a bug in the car."

When she pulled into the head of the driveway, they got out. Walking several feet, when Billy coughed and spit, saying, "What was that ungodly broth?"

"I don't know. Something that Pearl Jam and Criptin put together." "Yeah, lucky me, you had some mints in the car."

"You know Billy," she began, "For a while, I have been coming to hate this devil shit. At first, when I joined, I was into drugs big time, and I was always at the bank for money transfers. Being young and wild, I loved all the sex, gambling, and of course, all the drugs I wanted were at my disposal. I always half listened to the devil shit. Always wore a happy face. When I met Karen, and she thought I was a true believer, and then she convinced Criptin I would be a great society member of the inner circle. Then, I became part of the three-society witch's, that is head of thirty-two disciples. Of course,

I had lovers besides Vernon, that I was programmed to bring them in to the fold. The two that I seduced, became members and all they cared about, like the rest, was all the pleasures of life's good times. One of them is still there. Unfortunately, the others died from an overdose. That's where you came in. You're not like the rest. You were different. You didn't approach this cult shit as getting plenty of goodies, you seemed more like someone with hard questions. Billy, I am seeing now that this devil bullshit is a front to drugs, prostitution, racketeering and other things that they use to control me and others. So-called believers, people will believe anything if they are rewarded with things like drugs. People are just looking for any excuse to rob, steal, and do all kinds of nefarious things, without the fear of the law or God, and no guilt of the street's norms. Worship the devil, and you're on the right path."

"Wow, Cindy Lou. I would have never thought that's what you think."

"There's a room below, that I think inside, they are manufacturing drugs. For the outside, and of course, it's members. It's well guarded, but I believe it's a laboratory. It seems, they never run out of drugs for the members."

"What about Karen and Shara?" he asked.

"Forget about Karen, she's in it big time, and controlled by Red. Shara, I'm not sure about her, but Roland knows about her dating your brother. However, I don't trust any of them, and Vern is like a burning fuse. So, you going out with me, is extremely dangerous."

"Shit!" Billy exclaimed. "Could it be any more dangerous than this devil cult?"

Cindy took out her compact, when Billy said, "Why don't we go to the Rockville Police to investigate?"

"Are you kidding? That would be unwise, there are many members, that would unfortunately, greatly suffer and probably die if they were to be suddenly yanked from their drugs; and Criptin knows that. It has to be a well thought out plan that you and I Billy, wouldn't know where to begin."

Chapter 11

The next morning, Tess was preparing breakfast, when Rick said, "Mark, is Billy home?" Mark yawned, quipping, "Oh yeah, I didn't hear him come in through," then he added,

"Must have been in the wee hours."

Around eleven, Billy finally came down the stairs. Tess was preparing for a light lunch, when she looked up.

"Oh, Billy, my youngest twin of two minutes; you missed breakfast, but I am making ham and pickle sandwiches."

"Hey, that will work for me. Where's everybody?"

"Your father is finishing the repairs in the utility shed. Mark went off in his car."

Shortly after, Billy pitched in to help his father, until both parents left for town to straighten out a problem with the deed. When Mark drove up, Billy was thinking about what transpired the last month or so. A cold fear engulfed him. Mark parked, and walked over saying, "Billy boy, you look rather peaked. Tough night?"

"No, just my usual dose of loving, brother Mark." Then he added, "How's it going with Shara?"

"Not bad, but I planned to take her to the show last night, but she had to take her mother to Providence."

"Oh, really? How come?" "Visit a cousin."

Then, as Billy flashed back to Cindy Lou, Karen, and Shara and their disciples' robes; standing by the cauldron with a cup of that foul broth, that was supposedly ground up bloody tongues of burnt witches, from three or four hundred years ago. It made his stomach want to turn.

Mark half yelled, "Billy! What are you thinking about? You look like a ghost walked in front of you. You've got sweat running down your face."

"Oh, I was just thinking of Cindy Lou's boyfriend Vern, who could be gunning for me."

"I don't blame you," Mark put his spin on it. "I'm always looking over my shoulder for the likes of Roland."

"Yeah," Billy said, turning his thoughts into words, "What the fuck have we gotten into? Who would ever think so much drama in a one horse town?"

The next day, Cindy Lou called, and Billy left to meet her at Harry's Donuts, to talk about what they can do. Mark paced up and down, having a sort of melt down, thinking how he misses Shara; for unlike his brother who apparently has a sexual relationship with Cindy Lou. He's got it bad for the black eyes, black haired beauty from Peru.

So, within a few days, Mark called her to meet him after work at John Smally's in Rockville. She agreed, saying she would be there around 6:30, but on the side of caution, he might park his car behind a dumpster. He made sure Roland wasn't around to make a surprise showing. Then, he thought Billy was right, so much drama for a small town, but I will play my hand, as it goes with the beautiful Shara. Hopefully, it will be four aces, and not the dead man's hand. Aces and eights, with no sign of Roland, he drove into John Smally's, just as Shara was getting out of her car. His heart jumped, so to speak, when she stood by the door in a mini skirt, and a red top.

Mark called out, "Good to see you again." She smiled, "Likewise I'm sure."

Then, walking he said, "Whatever you want, I got it."

As they took a booth, Mark remarked, "How was Providence?"

"Alright, but I was glad to get back to the country. So, what have you been doing Mark?" "Well, actually I've been looking for work in Park City. I might start working at a dental office."

"Might?" Shara questioned.

"Yeah, because there's so much construction going on, a carpenter can almost pick anything, unless it's union."

"What about your brother?"

"I don't know. He better find something. Daddy-O sure is getting tired of lending him gas money."

They ordered, and Mark kept staring at her neck. Shara gave him a quizzical look.

"What are you looking at?"

He burst into laughter. "Sorry Shara, I was just thinking how I would love to plant my lips on your gorgeous neck."

"Oh Mark, you're something else. You always make me feel good."

He matched her smile, "That's how you make me feel."

Then, suddenly, the feel-good moments came crashing down, as Roland suddenly walked in. He looked around, then motioned Shara to join him. Seeing that she was getting up, "No," Mark said in a bluster, "Don't jump for him."

Shara put her hand on his shoulder, "Relax honey. I've got to talk to him for a few minutes."

Then, what seemed like an eternity, she rejoined him, as Roland gave him a cold, dirty look, and left.

"So," Mark questioned, "Are you still with him? Or am I just a second-rate boyfriend?" "It's okay Mark."

Trying to stall his anger, as the waitress brought over their food, Shara looked him in the eyes; "Honey, just be cool about it. He and his buddies aren't going to mess with you, if that's what you think."

"Shara," he responded, "I'm in it for the long haul. I'm just trying to wrap my arms around this whole thing with you and Roland. I know he's been paying your rent, but I ..."

Shara cut him off, "No, Mark. Not anymore. Not since I have opened the salon."

Mark responded, "Well okay, but I can help you and your mother out once I start working."

"Thanks honey, but like I said, the shop is beginning to realize a profit. So, I'm good." "Roger," then Mark voiced, "So, I gather you're going to keep quiet about your conversation with jerk-o?"

Shara clutched his hand, "Mark, please trust me on this."

He squeezed her hand tightly, saying, "Okay. I will."

It didn't however, shut down his thinking, of where did she get the money in the first place to buy the land, equipment, and all the expenses that come along when you open a new business. Was Roland more involved than she was saying? Does he even have a job?

Back at Harry's Donuts, Billy thought Mark and Shara have been there also. Rockville is so small, that it's the only coffee shop this side of town. Cindy Lou had a look of concern in her demeanor.

"Billy, I've found out a directive on the society secret web page, that the inner circle is calling for all members who are in the inner circle. That means me, Shara, and Karen, plus the thirty-two disciples plus the cult of the devil men's soldiers. Most of all, the younger men, that wear black cloaks of the devil symbols, must be there, including you."

"So, what do you think it's about?"

"Wait, Billy. There's more. One of the disciples, a woman that has been involved in this for several years ... I won't mention her name, except, that I ran into her a few months ago in Park City, and like myself, she's looking for a way to somehow escape what she calls a nightmare. She told me, a few years back, a young guy was planning to get out, but unfortunately told the wrong person. He was found in Bristol, Rhode Island, near where he's from, with a bullet in the back of his head. He was only twenty-five years old.

That's her biggest fear, that even if she slipped away, they would find her."

"Oh my God," Billy raised his voice, "You're talking about getting out. They could kill you."

"Relax, Billy. Cindy Lou's brain is working on a fool proof plan. But, for tonight, you're going to romp at my place." Billy got nervous now.

"I am wondering big time about Vern showing up."

"No chance," Cindy Lou elaborated, "Him and Red are at a monster truck competition over in Pacerville. But, for now my horny carpenter, I want you to nail me to the bed."

In a short time, Cindy Lou's Camry, and Billy's Camaro were parked side by side at her pad.

Mark returned to the farm, with more questions than answers after leaving Shara at John Smally's Diner. He knew she was holding back, in telling him what was really going on.

Meanwhile, the next morning, Cindy Lou and Billy emerged from her apartment, when she planted a long kiss as he got in his car.

"Wow," he felt wild gyrations like he did in bed, "That perfume you're wearing kills me; making it so I never want to leave."

Cindy Lou smiled, "It's Calvin Kline Escape. I'm glad you like it. I'll be in touch."

Billy backed out the driveway. On the way to the farm house, he suddenly noticed his wallet was missing. "Shit," he thought, "It must have fell out when I threw my pants on the chair."

Then, he opted to go back and get it. As he got closer, he thought the brown F150 parked in the driveway belonged to Red. Then, ditching the Camaro out of sight, he went around the back of the two-story apartment house, and snuck up the fire escape, when he heard a man yelling, and what sounded like Cindy Lou, in anguish. Through a space, where the shade wasn't exactly straight, he could see Vern and Red walking around Cindy Lou in the kitchen, who was seated in a chair. Red, was grilling her about being loyal to the society, then he heard Vern screaming at her about cheating on him with that "fucking carpenter." Then suddenly, Red produced a small knife, and then held it to her neck. Billy knew he left his hunting knife in the car!. Next, Billy heard Cindy Lou burst out in a short scream, then both men fled down the stairway to their truck. Billy could see that she was whimpering, as he banged on the back door. She was shocked to see Billy and embraced him. Then he could see a trickle of blood, running down her neck.

"What happened?"

He was seething with anger.

"Vern and Red say I have been ignoring the society websites, their blogs, emails, etc. Saying that I am not living up to my disciple privileges of the one of the three main inner circle witch disciples, because you're corrupting me."

Billy went to the sink, grabbing a washcloth, he applied it to her neck. She took the cloth, "It's just a scratch. They're trying to scare me." "You told me, that Vern wouldn't harm you."

"So, I thought. I think Red and the society are leaning on him big time." "So, what does that mean?" Billy asked.

"To prove my loyalty … I must do it through you."

Billy stepped back. "Through me?"

"It's okay Billy. I won't let it happen." "Tell me more Cindy."

"In our next rally, you well; must be tattooed, with Satan on your chest." Billy's mouth dropped, "What? Are you kidding me?!"

He walked around the kitchen, "And if I refuse?" "Never mind."

"Cindy Lou don't hold back."

"Like I said, no fucking way are you going."

"Cindy Lou, I can't hide, you know they would find me, or they would put the farm ablaze."

"No, I got a girlfriend in Vermont, we can hide out."

"No, Cindy. I'll have it done. They would eventually find us, and probably kill us." Cindy Lou put her head down. "I've got to think."

Billy knew things were now at a critical point.

"Tell me Cindy, what will happened if I refuse?"

Cindy Lou looked like a cold force invaded her persona. "Well," she shuttered, "They would take me to the room they call the circle of traders. There, I would be stripped, and all ten of the inner society soldiers would rape me, and the disciples would cut an upside-down crucifix on my shoulder."

"Oh my God," he half yelled, "These people are psychopaths and sickos. Come on, let me take you in my car, away from here for a while."

Cindy Lou agreed, saying, "Billy, it's my fault that you're involved in this shit. But, you're not going to have Satan on your chest."

"Why would they do these awful things to you? Just because you ignored the website?"

"Red and Vern, I am sure, told Criptin a lot of lies about me, that they're not mentioning." "Cindy, now I worry about Mark. Who are the highest disciples?"

"Well, I was. Along with Karen, and Shara."

"Oh my God," Billy cringed, "Would Shara carve a cross on your shoulder?"

"I don't know Billy. It all depends if they have gotten to her by brainwashing." "Cindy Lou," Billy said, "We must tell Mark."

"No, Billy! If Mark finds out she's involved, he may go ballistic and bring down the law, and God only knows who would be killed; including Shara."

"Honey," Billy chose his words carefully, "I'm going to go through with it, and have Satan on my chest."

"No way!" Cindy raised her voice. "No, you're not!"

"Look," Billy reminded her, "I already got two on my back. I'll just play along, then I'll regard it, as I am the big bad ass of the cult. You know of course, other people have gotten devil shit on their bodies. I've seen the bikers covered in that stuff. Nobody is going to rape and torture my girl."

"I understand how you feel, but I still don't want you to go through with it." "Case closed Cindy Lou. This meeting coming up, do you think it's connected?"

Cindy Lou lit a cigarette, "I think so. I just think, because Vern is so jealous, him and Red jumped the gun. I am sure at the meeting, they would threaten me, and then Red and Vern would get as semblance of revenge, by having you tortured, so to speak by having Satan on your chest." After riding around for a couple of hours, Cindy said, "My contact in Park City, and I have been working on a plan."

"Good Cindy Lou." Then he thought, she was in better shape than when he first found her in distress and crying.

They eventually went back to her apartment. Before she got out, Billy said, "Cindy, I never asked you. Do you work somewhere?"

She replied, that she sells housewares on the internet, but barely gets by and is deep in debt to Criptin's bank.

Billy laughed, "Cindy, my sexy woman. Will you sell me a butter dish?" "A butter dish? What on Earth for?"

"So, I can put some hot lotion in it and rub it all over your luscious body." "Ha! Billy, I hope you don't stay away too long."

"When is the meeting?"

"A week from Friday, the 9th."

"Well," Billy said, "This Friday, I'll be over to play house if you want." "You better come, my horny carpenter."

As Billy drove off, he yelled, "If those goons come back, call me! My old man has got a shotgun"

Chapter 12

On the way home, he got to thinking about Cindy Lou. For the first time in his life, he's got feelings for the opposite sex. Cindy Lou was much more than just some chick that he has sex with. Although, she has a big-time checkered past. I don't care, he thought. It's now when he is with her, that he feels wanted and needed, and her glowing smile is working its way into his heart.

Mark was sitting on the farmers porch when he drove up. "Well, brother Billy, another conquest of the opposite sex?"

"Ha, ha, very funny. What are you doing? Somebody said you were going to Park City to look for work."

"Yeah, well, that's on tomorrows agenda." Billy sat on the swing chair. "How's Shara?"

Mark grimaced, "I don't know. I just think she's holding back something from me," he then told him about how Roland came in to John Smally's.

"So, Mark, what do you really know about her?"

"Probably the same you know about Cindy Lou, who set you up for those tattoos."

Billy followed up, "You may not believe this, but I am starting to fall for the red head."

Mark thought, that was the last thing he thought he would hear. "I'm surprised," he replied.

"Remember Gail Beckman, in Pacerville? When you told me, you were crazy over her, until you found out she was married."

"Well, yeah, I was only nineteen. She played me, for mostly money, and promised me all kinds of things. Just giving me sex, while she was draining my bank account."

Mark laughed, "And always borrowing your old Chevelle SS, until you saw her driving around with an older guy, that turned out to be her husband."

"Alright Mark. Fuck off. Cindy Lou is different." Then, wanting to get back to Shara, he said, "Well, I must admit. Shara is one sexy, good looking broad. But, remember, Roland is her boyfriend."

"Not anymore," Mark raised his voice; almost like he was taking a victory walk. "Her and I are tight."

Billy slapped his brother, "Oh yeah? How tight is she?"

Cracking up, Mark pushed him, "Shut up, I haven't got that far yet." "So, when are you going to see her again?"" Billy questioned.

"I'm not sure, she's always working at her salon, and said something about she had to do something on the 9th."

Billy's mouth dropped, "What's going on the 9th?"

Mark stood up, "I wish I knew, but I haven't been dating her long enough to ask her too much of her personal business. Probably has to take her mother somewhere."

Billy then decided to raid the reefer for one of his father's beers. "You too?" He asked looking at his brother.

"Yeah, get me one."

Finally, that night, Billy laid in bed thinking about the last 24 hours, and now knowing that Shara is going to the meeting on the 9th, would she be that vile to cut Cindy Lou, along with Karen? After watching the perverts rape her? In his way of thinking, he must have the ugly tattoo on his chest done. At least, it would give Cindy Lou and her friend in Park City more time to put an end to this devil cult.

The next day, Cindy Lou left for Park City. Knowing a few years back, she had demonstrated some housewares at Carol Uxbridge's home. In fact, she took some with her, probably a little paranoid, in case she was followed. Hopefully, she would see Carol's tan Chevy Tahoe SUV in the driveway. She knew, that Carol wanted to talk further on somehow escaping the devil cult.

Carol was a forty-seven-year-old, divorced mother of two. She lived alone, and was originally from around the Richmond, Virginia area.

Seeing her car, Cindy Lou parked and knocked on the door. Carol was surprised and elated to see her. Cindy Lou knew she had to trust someone, for her options were few; and she told Carol what's been going down.

"Oh my God," Carol put her hands to her face. "What is it?" Cindy clutched her hand.

"My second year, that I was in the cult, I saw it firsthand. I was young, and impressed, and thought the church was just a made-up way to keep people from the truth of the Inquisition and the terrible wars of mankind, in the name of religion that went on for centuries. Criptin, the warlock, took me under his tutelage. Supposedly the truth of God vs Satan, and I saw a young woman, who somehow betrayed the inner circle of the cult. She was chained down, and raped by the society soldiers, then one of the three witch disciples, like you, Karen, and Shara; carved an upside-down crucifix not on her shoulder, but on her breast!. Then, Criptin said she would be taken back in the fold by atoning for her grievous sins against the Prince of Darkness. But, you know, I never saw her again. There was a rumor, that she was confined in a psychiatric clinic. Of course, nobody asked any questions; that was taboo. Just like now."

Cindy Lou then said, "I have a cousin on the Hartford, Connecticut police force. He's a lieutenant, but then again, it might not be a sound idea; it might be too risky. But Carol, my boyfriend Billy wants to go through with it to protect me."

Carol raised her eyebrows, "Boyfriend? I always thought Vern was your squeeze?"

"I've been over him for a while. Plus, Red cut me, and Vern enjoyed it. What can we do Carol?"

Carol sadly reflected, "Honey, I think the only way to take them down, is severing its tentacles."

"What do you mean?"

"Well, you know as well as I, that Criptin and his buddies have a clandestine operation of drugs, extortion, money laundering, protection, prostitution, and other nonferrous enterprises. If we could at least take one of them down, it would be a start."

Cindy Lou was overwhelmed with that reasoning. "Carol how could two women like us even know where to start?"

"Well, like you, that has connection to law enforcement in the lieutenant of the Hartford Police, I too have a son, that unfortunately, I have been estranged from for years, because of my young, stupid, anti-establishment mind."

Cindy asked, "Is he a cop?"

"More than that honey, he's a D.A. in Boston."

Cindy Lou couldn't believe it. "How long since you have talked to him?"

"A few years ago, at a funeral for an aunt. But you know, it's about time. Wouldn't you think?"

Then she got up, looking out the window. "That's the long part of it. But of course, I don't have a clue about the 9th. I hate to say this, but your boyfriend may have to have the tattoo on his chest."

"No!" Cindy Lou burst out. "There must be another way."

Carol went over and hugged her, "Believe me Cin, I wish there was. But, it will give us more time. I have some good tidbits for my son, if our reunion goes well. We must be extremely careful that our plans are kept secret. Even Billy shouldn't know."

"I understand Carol," taking in her caution.

Chapter 13

The next day, Rick and Tess, with their twin boys, were shooting the breeze on the porch, when Rick said, "Hey guys, my boss gave me four tickets to the Paw Sox. I thought we all might want to attend."

Tess perked up, "Sounds good honey. What do you think boys?" "It's Friday, the 9th," Rick added.

Mark said, "I'm in. Shara's going somewhere with her mother." Billy stood up, "Oh, I can't. Cindy Lou and I have a date."

Rick looked over, "Still playing with fire?" "No, I don't think so."

"Well," Tess regarded, "Honey, I am sure Billy has plans," her voice trying to cut through the tension.

"Okay then." Rick got up saying, "Tess, any coffee left in the pot?" Tess followed suit, "I'll fix you a cup."

After they went in to the house, Mark snickered, "So where are you taking your love bird for a date? Or is it just raw sex at her place?"

"Don't worry about it Mark. You just concentrate on your chick."

That night, Billy was once again with Cindy Lou, when he finally broke the silence about what's going to happen on the 9th. Cindy got up from the bed, slipping on her robe, "I tried a hundred times, to talk you out of going."

"No," Billy reiterated, "My mind is set in cement. You're not going to be cut."

Cindy Lou leaned over giving him a kiss, as he caressed her firm breasts. "Oh, Billy, you're a horny 24-year-old. We have already done it twice."

Billy smiled, "So, who's counting?"

"Come on," she nudged him from the bed, "I need a drink." She got him a beer, then made herself a Bloody Mary.

"Billy," she began, "Both you and I would stand before Criptin and the others, including the inner circle witches, and I would be read the bogus charges. That I haven't been focused, and been ignoring their emails, and not checking in with Criptin every month, to his witch craft meeting. Which, I have been ignoring, to a certain extent. However, I think Red and Vern set me up for something that I have done, which is of course a fucking lie. It's a way for Vern to get back at me because of you. They would tell you, that if you have Satan on your chest, I would be spared, and you would be a full-fledged, accepted member. By showing your love of Satan.

Then, Criptin and that other idiot Pearl Jam, would say if you refused, you know what will happen to your girlfriend. Then, he would say, no matter what happens, I would be shunned of any further participation in the inner circle."

"Who is this Pearl Jam? Why does he call himself that?

"Because, he's a complete psychopath. He thinks that naming himself after an iconic band, it will adhere to the members, but the truth is, he's an animal. Once, he beat a member so hard with his gold cane, that the person has brain damage."

"Boy, this devil shit sounds like a vicious gang of outlaw bikers."

"Worse than that Billy. It must be taken down."

Billy got up, looking into a small mirror hanging in the kitchen, "So what's one more?

I've seen plenty of devil tattoos. I can handle it."

Then he went over, giving her a big hug. Placing her hand, on his hard cock, she cracked up, as he picked her up saying, "Come on baby. I just love red heads."

In the bedroom, he crawled between her legs, curling her pubic hairs saying, "No doubt honey, you're a true red head!"

After more torrid love making, Cindy Lou went into his arms. "Billy," she softly said, "Ya know, I'm getting pretty fond of you. At first, I thought you were an asshole, but I have pretty much changed my opinion. Not only of you, but my whole wasted life in this devil shit. When I brought you to the first rally, I was not so much a believer in Satan, I was into the bank, and I knew I could always have access to money, and the drugs that I got hooked on. That was, until a couple members died from over doses, then, I got clean. I participated in group sex, along with Karen, who to this day, her and Red do lines and other stuff. The first couple years was like living in Candy Land. Everything was at your taking. You always turned a blind eye to all the tell-tale signs of rackets, that Criptin and the so-called society members were networking. Billy, most of the inner circle live in million-dollar houses, have wives, and some cases husbands or boyfriends, that are oblivious to what's going on. Somehow, they hide the operations through dark channels, that law enforcement, the DEA and the IRS are unable to make a connection. Just stay strong honey, and we will both get through this."

Billy said, "Cindy, why do they use this devil thing in the first place?"

"Because, if people believe there's no God, no accountability, and Criptin drills it into their minds, that under Satan's watch, you do whatever the fuck you want, and sometimes, that even includes murder.

July 8th rolled around eventually, and Mark took Shara to the super market for groceries in his SUV. In the market, he could see Shara buying a lot of Spanish food, saying, "Honey, isn't a lot of Spanish food loaded with salt?"

She responded, "Yes and no. It all depends on how you cook it."

In the cereal aisle, Shara bent over for a box of Grape nut cereal, and Mark focused on her butt, as she was wearing yoga pants. Noticing, she turned saying, "Mark, I close the salon at 5:30 tonight. Why don't you stop by at 6:30?"

Mark squinted his eyes, then in a sexy voice added, "I have a comfortable couch in my office."

At the farm house, Mark took a long shower. Then, applying McGraw cologne, he put on some fresh duds. Billy noticed saying, "Well Mark-O, looks like a hot date for you tonight."

"Could be." Then he jumped in his SUV to Shara's salon.

At the same time, Cindy Lou got Carol Uxbridge's phony request in an email to bring over some previously talked about housewares. After a few hours drive, Cindy Lou was at Carol's house. Inside, their orchestrated meeting went as planned. Cindy Lou was extremely happy that Carol and her son had finally buried the hatchet and enlightened him about the goings on and to investigate the crime rackets disguised as a devil's cult, as if it was play actors in Summer Stock. Then, Carol added, that her son Rob was also getting together a task force to investigate the information that she gave him, and pertinent evidence that the last two rally's that she wired herself.

"No," Cindy Lou was suddenly distressed, "These monsters would kill you. That's probably after they tortured you first. You took an awful risk."

"I know honey, but these perverts, for lack of better word, must be brought to justice. Is Billy prepared for the ceremony?" "Yeah, he says he is."

"Well then, maybe you should head home."

"You're right, we shouldn't be seen together. I don't know if they remembered I sold housewares. However, I'll see you tomorrow night, and be careful Carol."

She assured Cindy Lou she would be.

Then Cindy headed back to Rockville.

Friday night, the 9th, arrived quickly, and Cindy Lou picked up Billy and they arrived at the cult. Before long, all the inner circle members were filing in, as the regular members wouldn't be there. They all took seats, along with the society members, the officers, and the disciples, as well as the soldiers and Criptin and Pearl Jam.

The usual protocol, having Billy blindfolded, then it was removed. He and Cindy Lou stood before Criptin's inner circle. Criptin, along with several older, gray-haired men, and a few witches, were seated in chairs, when Criptin spoke of a list of charges.

"Cindy Lou Morgan, this board finds some serious accusations. That you have not been responding to our websites, ignoring texts and blogs, haven't contributed to the fund in three months, have continued running up high debts from our bank. However, two of my most trusted soldiers, Red and Vern have said that you are trying to subvert this organization through miss deeds inclusive not of a high disciple. You're cahooting with a new member, gives us serious concern. Although, taking another is no big deal, but because he is a neophyte, and Vern says you're sounding belligerent on your role; he thinks you want out because of your new boyfriend. What do you say about these charges?"

"Not true Criptin of the order of the Devil. I just got lax, not anything that I couldn't rectify. Although I have a new boyfriend, I still swear allegiance to the society. My old boyfriend pumped up these charges, because he's jealous, and it's totally off the wall that I have been trying to subvert the order."

"The die has been cast," Criptin said, looking over to Karen and Shara, and a new inner society witch.

"Will you, Billy Martin, have a tattoo of the Prince of Darkness, the true force, on your chest?"

"Yes, sir."

"Good," Criptin elaborated, "Please remove your shirt, and sit in the chair just off the trader's circle. You Cindy Lou Morgan, will be stripped of your rank as a high inner circle disciple, and reduced to just a member."

As Billy waited in the chair, he could see Shara and Karen in their seats, and what he saw next, put a cold shiver down his spine. Lying next to Shara, was a small, but nasty little pearl handled knife, that apparently was going to be used on Cindy Lou's shoulder if he refused to have Satan on his chest. Then, a tall man entered the ceremony carrying a bevy of tattoo paraphernalia in a suitcase, removing the loaded-up dye. In just under an hour, he was finished. Billy got up, his chest burning. In the mirror, the ugly profile of Satan himself!

Soon, Criptin held up the gavel saying, "Brothers and sisters, soldiers and witches; Billy Martin is now a full pledged member. We are now adjourned." Cindy Lou and Billy quickly got into her Blue Camry. "Are you okay Billy?"

"Just take me back to your place."

At the same time, Mark was on the computer learning about the country of Peru. He was constantly thinking about last night, when he and Shara made love for the first time. He then said to himself, "I'm going to marry that girl, or I will die trying."

Back with Cindy Lou and Billy, she pulled into her digs, then they went upstairs. Billy just collapsed in a chair saying, "Honey, how long before I can take a shower?" "Three or four days. I wouldn't get it wet."

Billy grimaced.

Reading his concern, she kissed him. "Don't worry darling, I'm going to give you a sponge bath."

"What? Are you sure?"

"Do frogs croak? Now lose your clothes and get in the tub." As she was sponging him, he was quiet.

"What are you thinking about?"

"Just how lucky I am to have you."

"No, Billy boy. I'm lucky to have you. Who else would have done that to help a former, disciple witch?"

Then, suddenly from under the suds, up popped his penis.

She laughed, saying, "No Billy,"" and then she pushed it down. Then in the following second, he grabbed her into the tub, clothes and all. She managed to get back up and stripped off her clothes. "Oh, what the hell. I might as well join you now."

Chapter 14

Back at the farm, Rick calls Peaceful Acres, Rick and Tess were drinking high balls. Tess looked over to her husband, "Well Honey, both boys now have girlfriends."

"Yeah. I just hope they know what they're doing in lieu of how they nearly got beat up."

Tess responded, "You would think they would bring them over to meet us."

"That, I don't think will happen too quickly. Especially Billy, since she probably set him up for those tattoos on his back."

"Well," Tess elaborated further, "Mark is on the computer, so Billy must be on a date with, I think he calls her Cindy Lou."

Rick cupped his chin, "Yeah, Tess, I wonder why she always picks him up?" Tess laughed, "Probably doesn't want to get the Camaro dirty."

"Well, I don't know Hon, that car was always what he calls a chick magnet. It just seems strange."

"A couple of weeks ago," Tess said, "Mark told me about his current girlfriend. That, she's from Peru in South America."

"Really?" Rick quipped. "What else did he say about her?"

Tess suddenly broke out in a warm smile and chuckled, "He told me, Mom, she seems as pure as the fallen snow, and probably walks around an insect so she doesn't step on it."

That night, the land line rang, and Tess answered.

"Oh, hi Mom. It's Billy. Just wanted to tell you and Dad, that me and Cindy Lou are going camping in New Hampshire for a week."

Surprised, Tess came back, "But honey, do you even have any camping equipment?"

"Oh, don't worry mom, Cindy Lou has everything. I just wanted you to look after my baby for me."

"Okay son," Tess replied, "Will do, and be careful. Call me when you get there okay?" "Okay mom. See you soon."

However, Billy and Cindy Lou weren't going camping, but to Carol Uxbridge's house in Park City. When they arrived, Carol ushered them to the back deck. Cindy Lou knew she had some new developments. They took seats around a small table.

"Billy," Carol said, "Take off your shirt."

Billy kind of stalled until Cindy Lou nodded. He stood up, as Carol examined the tattoo. "You did a brave thing Billy, in what would have been a horrible nightmare for your girlfriend."

"I know," Billy agreed quietly.

Then, Carol gave a little information, that her son was gathering all stop's in a plan to take down, essentially a crime syndicate. Billy's mouth dropped, and Cindy Lou told him that's all he should know for now.

Billy voiced, "Why? You can't trust me?" "We do!"

She got up, giving him his shirt, and planted a kiss. "We both know that now, but for the sake of caution, it's best that you don't know. But, Billy, we are hopefully going to take down these motherfucking, sick, anti-Christ scumbags."

"Wow!" Billy said. "You did turn the corner."

"That I did hon. Like I told you before, I was just confused. Easily targeted because of my obsession for drugs."

Carol spoke up, "Me too Billy. I couldn't function without an everyday fix. If that meant worshiping the so-called devil, so that I could get my candy, than so be it."

Cindy Lou added, "Honey, you and your twin, to the society, seemed like easy pickings for guys your age. A lot are into lines or pills or liquor. However, after Jimmy's Bar, we reported, I am sorry to say now, that you, not your brother, was potentially a good candidate for membership. I guess Criptin and his band of fuck faces didn't think that some guy's would want to work like you carpenters, for an honest day's wage. Karen and I thought you were into this stuff."

"And don't worry," Carol perked up, "When this nightmare is over, I know someone who will remove the tattoos. So, I'm glad I got you guys for a week. It's been a while since my boyfriend Tony and I split. It will be nice to have some company."

"Yeah," Cindy Lou breathed, "Billy had to get away from his folks, until we can somehow think of why he was tattooed again. He is worried his father would kick him out."

"Well, yeah," Billy responded, "But, I worry about Mark dating Shara. Just watching her sitting there at the meeting, it was like she was enjoying it. And right beside her was a knife to cut Cindy Lou if I refused."

"No, honey," Cindy Lou interjected.

, I was watching her. There really was no emotion," Billy said. "Regardless, I wouldn't trust her as far as you could throw her."

Cindy Lou thought, "Carol, do you know her at all?"

Carol poured herself a cup of coffee, "Not really. I could see how you, Karen, and her were quickly elevated to the top three witches' disciples."

Cindy Lou got up and poured herself cup also, saying, "You're right Carol. We did. For me, it was of course all about more tidbits, meaning better access to drugs and the bank. As far as Shara is concerned, I honestly never saw her use drugs, but she was at the bank a lot, and Roland was her lover. As far as Karen goes, she was a big drug user, and it was rumored, she was sucking Criptin's cock."

Carol piped up, "I heard that rumor too."

Billy shook his head, "So do you women think Shara is playing my brother?" Cindy Lou was borderline, and Carol had no idea.

Chapter 15

The next day, Mark called Shara at work, asking if she could get away for a rock concert in Boston in a couple of weeks. She told him she would let him know. Mark then thought, almost every time he asked her to go somewhere, she most always stalls. He wondered sometimes if Roland was really in the picture still or not.

Back at Carol's place, while Billy was cat-napping, Carol told Cindy Lou about her son's task force. That working with the law enforcement agencies is nicely coming together.

"That's great Carol. Those scumbags need a lesson in decency."

"Another thing," Carol gleaned, "Did you know that the caves where we hold our meetings, are part of a labyrinth? That spider webs underneath area that is quite intensive."

"I never knew that."

Carol smiled, "Yeah, well, when I first got married, and the kids were small, I got interested in Geology. I kept a lot of the area's topographic maps of the areas underground. Although, I lived in Park City like I said, this area underneath Rockville, there's a lot of tunnels as far as I can ascertain. In fact, it's probably why they named the town Rockville."

Cindy suddenly thought, the meetings are not that far from the Martin Farm. She got excited, "Carol, do you think the caves continue for quite a distance?"

"I don't know, but that's a good point. I am going to try and dig them up tonight. They're 1971 prints. I don't think I threw them away."

"Also," she said, "Cindy do you know the disciple's sister's Shirley and Patty Hokem?" Cindy Lou thought, "I'm not sure. There are 32 disciples. Why? What about them?" "Well," Carol began, "In the last few months, I've noticed they are becoming put off by this devil crap. Although, they haven't said anything. I can tell by their mannerisms. I know it's kind of flimsy, but they might be another crack in Criptin's Devil Cult."

"Where do they live?"

"I think over in Pacerville."

So, Cindy Lou continued, "What I should I do with Billy? He doesn't want to go home. I really think he's kind of traumatized by the tattoo. I'm afraid if he stays at my place, Vern is so vicious that he might try something beyond the pale. This so-called New Hampshire is only for a week."

"I know," Carol retorted, "I've been trying to gin up something, but am stumped." Thinking about their conversation, Cindy Lou suddenly remembered, "I saw Patty Hokem getting drugs, as I was smoking cocaine. We were shooting the breeze, when she told me she used to go out with Eddie Fenstermaker, whom I knew; but anyways, like us, she couldn't get enough of the candy. She wouldn't give all of it up."

"Honey," Carol conveyed, "People can change. Look at us. Anyways, in two weeks, is the next meeting, maybe I can find out more about the Hokem sisters."

Back at the Martin farm, around 11:30pm, Mark kept thinking about how Shara could sometimes be mysterious, and for some reason, he jumped into his SUV and drove to the salon. Then, cutting his lights, he saw the Ford F150 parked out front right next to her car. A dim light could be seen from her office. He was livid. That's probably where she's screwing Roland. Unable to control his anger, he parked behind the dumpster, then stole up behind the pickup, and took pictures of the back of the truck and registration plate, with his cell phone. Could it be Red he thought? It was his truck. Or, maybe there's a gang-bang going on!

What seemed like a dagger being plunged into his heart, he retreated to his SUV, and though he felt like smashing the door, his senses returned. He has pictures, and one thing is for certain he thought, I won't be sleeping tonight.

After a week of staying at Carol's house went by, Cindy Lou and Billy headed for the farm. Cindy Lou stopped at the head of the driveway said, "Are you sure?"

Billy eyed her sexy shorts and halter top, leaning over and giving her a tantalizing kiss, "I'm sure."

Then he walked to the house and noticed all the vehicles were in the yard. He saw Mark and their father painting one of the barns.

Seeing Billy, Mark said, "Hey! How was New Hampshire?" "Great," Billy reiterated.

Rick said, "How's the girlfriend?" "She's okay."

Mark then said, "You're in luck, there's plenty of bacon left over. Mom will probably make you a B.L.T."

Billy rubbed his eyes, "All I want is some shut eye. It was a long trip back." Rick and Mark came in, when Tess called them in for lunch.

Rick said, "Where's wild son Billy?"

"Oh," Tess explained, "He wanted to hit the hay and he said he has a hell of a headache." Rick sneered, and Mark tried to smooth it over.

"Well Dad, he loves to paint, I'm sure when he feels better, he will pitch in."

After lunch, Rick and Mark went and worked on the barn the better part of the afternoon. Billy never came downstairs to pitch in.

Rick commented, "Looks like I am down to one son."

Mark, knowing it hasn't been going too well with them because of the recent past said, "No big deal Dad, he's probably hung over." Rick looked disgusted, saying, "Yeah, hangover my ass! That red-headed bitch is an albatross around his neck." Then he walked away.

Around 11:30pm, Mark went upstairs to turn in, and noticed his brother was laying on the bed in his shorts, but also had his shirt on despite the heat and the lone fan. Mark cranked the fan to full power, when Billy looked over.

"Tough week with the chick?"

"In a way," Billy lied, "We partied with her friends in Goffstown. You know me, can't leave the booze alone."

Mark then hit the pillow.

Chapter 16

The next morning, Mark saw Billy was still asleep, and found it rather peculiar that Billy still had his shirt on in the stifling heat. He soon found out why though, when Billy rolled over, and he saw the Satan Devil tattoo.

"Oh my God!" Mark exclaimed.

Billy heard the outburst and stood up. "Looks like you saw the tattoo." Mark shook his head. "What the hell?!"

Billy put a robe on and went to take a shower. Rejoining his brother, he said, "You still here?" Then he said, "Cindy Lou didn't know that the party was ripe with cocaine. Some were doing lines, smoking crack. Then, everybody paired off for sex. The last thing I remember, I passed out, and somebody said I was so fucked up, that I told them I wanted another tattoo. But, I didn't want Satan, that's for sure."

"Why would they do that?" "They're fucked up people."

Mark said, "Where was your girlfriend?"

"She went off the wagon, she thinks someone slipped her a Quaalude or something. She passed out and she thinks someone was trying to take her pants off."

Mark walked over to the window, looking out, "It sounds like a fantasy story. Almost like you're putting me on."

Billy shot back, "Oh, it happened alright. Why would I get the devil on my chest after getting witchcraft hexes on my back? Both me and Cindy Lou were out of it."

Mark came across, "You have had nothing but trouble since meeting that snatch!"

"Easy," Billy put his hand up, "She's not perfect, but I like her."

Mark elaborated, "Actually, we have had nothing but heartache, since we met these broads. I think Shara is cheating on me."

"You're kidding." Billy acted surprised. "After all the bragging about her?"

Mark, in a look of gloom, went right to the part about Red's pickup in the driveway around midnight.

"Hey brother, that doesn't mean anything, maybe she had a problem with the A.C., or some other maintenance issue. Cindy Lou told me that Red works for a heating and A.C. contractor."

Mark then considered what he said, "Well then, what does that asshole Roland do?" Billy buffed his shoes, "I don't have a clue."

Back at Carol Uxbridge's, Carol got into the Chevy Tahoe SUV and lit out to join her son in a preordained meeting in an out of the way coffee shop, on the edge of Park City. Her son was already there, as she knew that the black unmarked late Ford Vic was his. She pulled in and joined him. Her oldest son, Rob Sergi, a, imposing man, in a smart apparel, was equipped with a tape recorder, and told his mother to tell anything she knew about the cult.

Back in Rockville Billy was with Cindy Lou in her apartment.

"The meetings tomorrow night, are you going to be okay honey?" Then she elaborated, "Make sure you show Criptin, Pearl Jam, and their buddies your Satan tattoo. Kind of like you're bragging about how it stands out and all. That could be a silver lining in all this shit."

"What do you mean?" Billy looked perplexed.

"They would trust you more and that could be helpful, when Carol, at some point drops the gauntlet. But, for now, Mr. William Martin, we're going to do sixty-nine, then you're going to fuck my brains out!"

Billy laughed, "That's the best thing I've heard since wheat germ was invented." Cindy Lou's mouth dropped, "wheat germ invented? What are you talking about?'

Billy laughed again, "When I was a teenager, my great Uncle Henry told me to eat plenty of wheat germ, and the ladies will never complain."

This time, Cindy Lou broke out in a tirade of laughter, "Is Henry still around?" "I think so, I never heard that he had passed."

"Good," she said, "Because I want to give him a medal." This time, they both laughed.

Chapter 17

The next night, Cindy Lou and Billy arrived at the check point. They were quickly in the meeting room. Billy could see it was rather packed, as he wondered how so many people really believe in this bullshit. Criptin, in his usual welcome ceremony, and the praising of the devil and the witches, now and before the Burning Times. Then of course, people went to their special rooms, for gambling, sex, drugs, and to get money from the bank. Some went to the carved-out log, that was a bar with hex symbols embedded on the top, that's where Billy went.

But, before everyone left, Criptin told them he'd be back for a disciplinary hearing of a member. Everyone knew, that when Criptin put out a directive, that it was carved in stone. Cindy Lou, now reduced to only a regular disciple, kind of grimaced when she heard that Billy had a whiskey sour.

The hour passed, and Billy downed 3 sours. Then everyone came back to the meeting room, as again Criptin took center stage in his winged cloak.

"Cult members, once again, in honor of paying tribute to Satan and our sister witches, there has been a crack in the security. A young woman member has been found to bring attention to the cult. This information has come to me. She was high on drugs, when she told a police officer in Central Falls, Rhode Island, near where she lives, about our sacred rituals. I am told, the cop didn't believe her, but the point is, she crossed the line."

Then he motioned for her to stand in front of the jeering body. The woman, probably not more than twenty years old, in what looked like a white paper shift, with long brown hair, was asked by Criptin, "Do you Allison, deny these charges?"

"No Criptin," she cried out, "But I was spaced out on crack and pills. I don't remember." "Well," Criptin said, as he walked in front of her, "Two cult members were with you as witnesses, and it has been verified. So, you must be punished."

"No! Please Criptin, no!" she yelled.

Then, in a flash, he tore off her flimsy, thin shift. In shock, she covered her breasts with one hand, while covering her genitalia with the other. Then, at that moment, Billy saw Red and Vern grab her arms. Criptin, then went into a sickening spiel about after life, paranormal, 666, Satan, Anti-Christ venom, and of destroying him. As the girl wept, "Allison!" Criptin called out. "You have three options, that you must choose from. Number one, that your stash of drugs, will be taken away when you leave."

"No, no," she cried, "Please not that. I need my drugs, I can't live without them. Please, no!." I can't function without the drugs, I must have them!

"The second option have one of your big toe-nails ripped off, as a penance to the almighty Satan."

"No," she yelled.

"The third option is, you will be taken to the circle of traders, where you must give oral sex to ten inner circle soldiers."

Allison put her hand up, "Please, I was out of my mind on crack and pills. That is why I supposedly told the cop."

"Supposedly shit!" Criptin suddenly slapped her, and she whimpered. "So what decision will it be Allison. Take away your drugs? Lose a toe-nail? Damn," Criptin cringed, "That sounds like a lot of pain. But of course, that sounds like a walk in the park, compared to what happened to our sisters of Satan who were stretched on racks, viciously whipped, and torn with red hot pincers. Then, of course, is the third option. However, since it's your first offense, you will only give five soldiers oral sex. So, which will it be Allison?"

"Please, no Criptin. Please spare me."

"Which one Allison!?" Criptin said in a forceful tone.

Allison was beyond traumatized, as balls of sweat rolled off her body. Stuttering, then pointing to the Circle of Trader's Red and Vern roughly pushed her to the middle of the burning candles, where five inner society soldiers waited. Vern and Red forced her to her knees, then one by one, each soldier lifted their cloaks. Billy looked away in disgust, knowing there were probably a lot of members that were so hooked on drugs, that they would do things so revolting, to get what Cindy Lou called their candy.

The rest of the night, the members then drifted off to their poisons. Finally, he met Cindy Lou at the check point, where he showed an inner circle member his Satan tattoo, and the man congratulated him. On the way back, Cindy Lou didn't say much. When Billy told her that the punishment the young girl went through has really cut into him like a hot knife.

She grabbed his hand, "Honey, let's hope that it won't be too long before they are destroyed." Then, Cindy Lou highlighted, "Did you see Shara at all?"

"No," he answered, "She wasn't with Karen or the new girl."

"I know," Cindy Lou looked concerned, "I wonder why she wasn't there."

Billy thought, "Well, being a Thursday, aren't the meeting usually on Fridays?"

"That's right but, Criptin called it earlier because of all the Allison stuff happening. But, all member gets emails, so I am sure Criptin and Pearl Jam must be looking for her."

Chapter 18

In Park City, Mark and Shara pulled into a Mexican Restaurant. Shara gleaned, "Mark, you could have chosen American Food."

"Don't worry about it Shara," he responded, "Hey, I like Mexican too."

He never said too much about what had transpired since their last date.

Taking seats, she looked stunning in a red flower print dress, and matching top, and white flat shoes. He long, black hair was braided, and she wore red polish on her nails. A medallion of some symbol hung around her neck.

So, Mark, taking it all smiled. "Shara, so how's the salon going?"

"Great!" She smiled back, "Thanks for asking. We're starting to realize a profit." Then they ordered, when Mark went back to the topic of the salon.

"How old is that building anyway?"

"Oh," Shara fussing with her eyebrows, "So, they tell me it's quite old. Someone said it was built in 1913, It was a consignment shop at one time."

"Does the A.C. work good?"

"No, not really. I had to have it repaired not too long ago."

Mark knew asking too many questions might tip her on his intent.

"Well, I know one thing my black-haired beauty; I'm glad it was okay when I was with you in your office."

Shara, with a million-dollar smile, laughed. "Right, or we both would have been melted."

Then Mark asked her, "What's it like in Peru?"

"It's a pretty country, but for the most part, people are poor. The highlight was when my eight-grade class all went to the once lost Inca City of Machu Picchu."

"Hey," Mark breathed, "That's so cool. I've heard about that place."

"Yeah, it was breath taking." And you know what else?"

Mark said, "You're breath taking. So, my Peruvian girlfriend, what do you want to do after we eat?"

She looked into his eyes and she could see the look of a handsome man with sexual overtones.

"So, what do you have in mind?"

"Well," he said, "It's such a beautiful evening, with such a beautiful girl, it seems it would be a waste if we didn't make love."

Shara giggled again, "You know Mr. Mark, I was supposed to go visit a girlfriend in Park City, but I canceled to be with you, because I wanted you to hold me as tight as you can." "Wow!" Mark ratched up his answer, "Honey, I think I am frozen, can you help me out?" She laughed as the waiter brought the check.

So, Mark said, "What do you think of my idea?"

"The only thing honey, being so late, my mom would be waiting up for me. She gets nervous, because in the Bronx in New York, there was a guy trying to follow me, and for a while I wouldn't go anywhere walking. There are sections that are extremely dangerous."

Mark then suggested, "Call her and tell her you are going to be late." "Okay, then where are we going?"

"Just six miles down the road, there's the Rose Flowered Motel."

"Oh really, Mr. Mark. Have you been there before?" "No, not at all. I saw it on the Park City website."

"Mark honey, my mother is probably, what some American's would say, is from the Ice Age. The best I can see us there for, is less than two hours. Do you want to spend money on that short amount of time?"

He leaned over, clutching her hands, "Baby, I wouldn't care if it was only five minutes." "Okay. I'm game."

Inside the motel, Mark shed his duds, and jumped in the bed, waiting for her to emerge from the bathroom. She was clad in a red bra, and red thong. Quickly, he kissed her all over. Then, as she was whimpering, he slid down her body, removing the bra and thong, then he curled her pubic hair, before he entered her with his tongue. He could hear her moaning in quick outbursts, as he kept twisting and probing.

"Oh, Mark," she cried out, "I love you," escaped from her lips.

Finally, he slipped his cock in and they rocked back and forth. She let loose with broken words and just long sighs, until they climaxed simultaneously. For the first time, Mark had oral sex with her, and she kept hugging him, saying, "Mark, please stay with me, no matter what I have done."

"What do you mean my beautiful Peruvian?"

Then, her cell rang. It was her mother asking her to pick up some milk.

After all that, and driving to Rockville forty-five minutes from the city, he dropped her off. He kept thinking about what she had done. He didn't want to bring it up again, for it might put a sour note on a beautiful night.

On the way to the farm he kept thinking, Is Roland still coming around? They had previously agreed to go fishing in four days.

Chapter 19

At Carol Uxbridge's house, Cindy Lou and Billy were drinking Bloody Mary's on the deck, when Carol joined them.

"I just talked to Mr. S, and things are really heating up." "Good," Cindy Lou responded.

Billy knew, that the plan to take down Criptin was coming together. Carol, then broke out an old topographic map of the underground areas of Rockville.

"In the last few days, I have been going through it with a fine-toothed comb. Where the caves are, where the cult has set up their secret hideaway. It goes half a mile in one direction, before spreading out to off shoots." Then she hesitated, and looked at Billy motioning him over, "Look at this."

Billy focused, but it didn't seem to register.

Carol pointed out, "See this tiny blue line? That's a stream of water that goes within an eighth a mile from your farm."

"Carol, we were looking for an underground well somewhere on the property when my parents first bought the farm. Would it be on the map?"

"No, but I am willing to bet the water from the stream, it would support a well somewhere on the property."

Then Carol retreated to the kitchen.

"Hold on guys, I'll make us some sandwiches."

Soon, all were digging into delicious ham and cheese on rye, with tomato and lettuce.

Billy quipped, "I never knew why they called them sandwiches. It seemed like a crazy name for food."

Cindy Lou smiled, "Billy boy, I learned that in school." "Then enlighten me Professor Cindy Lou Morgan."

"Ha, ha, very funny. There was a guy in England who had a title, The Earl of Sandwich. You know how the English love their titles. Well, the earl was a heavy gambler. One day, when the cook tried to coax him to the dining room to eat, he was so involved in his gambling, that he simply told the cook to put the meat between two slices of bread, and hence forth, you have the sandwich."

Carol laughed, "It's strange how some things get named. Annie Oakley for one, was such a marksman, that Sitting Bull, the Sioux chef, named her Little Miss Sure Shot."

Billy laughed, "We need a hundred Annie Oakley's to take down Criptin and his pals."

"Don't worry," Cindy Lou highlighted, "It's coming."

Then Carol said, "On a more serious note, I have talked to the Hokum sisters. I think we can trust them. Shirley, I'm totally sure about, but Patty, she's like we once were. Hooked on the candy."

Cindy Lou voiced, "That's a problem. Remember Allison wouldn't give up her candy for anything and sucked five cocks in front of the body."

Billy let out a disgusted sigh, "That was beyond gross. Red and Vern were holding her too."

Chapter 20

The next morning, at the Martin Farm, as autumn started its transformation to the bright colored leaves; Tess joined her husband and Mark on the porch.

"I had to put on a sweater. It's getting mighty chilly."

"Yeah Mom. Fall can be chilly, but it can be followed by a brutal winter."

"We should be good," Rick added, "With the plow on the new truck, we should be golden."

"Oh, Dad, next Monday, I start a job in Park City; working for Lane Construction, on an office building."

Rick thought, then said, "Lane Construction, I heard they have a good reputation. They did a post office in Boston several years ago. I knew the clerk of the works."

Mark further said, "I'm sure I can get Billy a job."

Tess, sipping her coffee, looking out at the brilliant colors, kind of gave a sigh, "I wish he would stay home long enough to let us know what he's doing."

Rick laughed, "Yeah, no shit. Ever since he met that Cindy girl, you never know what he's getting into."

"And you Mark," Tess came across, "When are you going to bring your girlfriend home to meet us?"

"Soon Mom. I promise."

In a few days, Mark and Shara went to a small pond to fish. However, they didn't have a fishing license, but they took a chance. They packed a lunch, they fished, and had a fabulous time. But, gnawing on Mark's mind, was her comment about staying with her no matter what she had done. So, before they left, he brought it to center stage, so to speak.

"Oh," she was kind of embarrassed, "I just hope you will forgive me for being part of the trap with Red, Vern, and Roland, and playing you along at Jimmy's Bar."

"You mean that's all?" Mark grinned. "Okay my Shara, you must pay a penalty for getting me all hot and bothered."

Shara looked, as his mischievous tone was radiating into more than just fishing. The proof was when he walked over. She could see a push on his pants. She smiled, reaching down squeezing.

"So, what's my penalty Mr. Martin?"

"See that small berm of grass?" he said pointing. "Yes, Mr. Martin. It looks all soft and cuddly." "Well, do I have to say any more?"

"Don't you think it's kind of chilly to disrobe?" she laughed.

He picked her up, all 108 pounds of her, and walking to the berm he said, "I promise to keep you warm and cuddly, and I also promise that I will love you like you've never been loved before."

All Shara did, was let out a long pleasurable sigh.

Meanwhile, Billy and Cindy Lou, left Park City, returning to drop off Billy. Then, reminding him of the society meeting in the next couple of weeks, she told him, that Carol was going to Pacerville to talk to the Hoken sisters; to see if they are going to be 100% on board with the plan to take down the cult.

Billy thought, "What the hell can they do?" "We will leave it up to Mr. S and Carol." Soon, Billy was back at the farm.

"Will I see you tonight Billy boy?"

All Billy said was, "I'll be there faster than Dale Earnhart Jr. going for the pole."

And all Cindy Lou said was, "Whatever that means. The only thing I can glean from that, is I want your pole."

They both cracked up in laughter as Billy got out of the car throwing her a kiss.

Over the next two weeks, Mark would meet Shara at the salon once it closed. Usually on a Tuesday or Thursday, to get a bite to eat at John Smally's. In the restaurant one night, Mark told her of a certain play that's coming to Providence, that he knows she wanted to see, it was on Friday the 12th.

"Oh Honey," Shara looked over in disappointment, "I can't make it. I have plans to go to Pacerville to a friend that is a buyer of new hair products. She always gives me a cut on the price."

"Damn, that's too bad babes. But, I suppose you're keeping up with the latest fads." She smiled, "Exactly, but I want to go at some point."

As they went to their vehicles, Shara asked him if he would mind taking a couple of boxes from the back seat to the trunk. She told him they are discontinued products that she will sell to a couple of girlfriends at dirt cheap prices.

When Mark removed them from the back seat to move them to the trunk, he noticed the Buick Regal had a so-called escape latch, that one could get out if they were accidentally locked in.

"So," Mark embraced her, "Saturday night, do we get together?"
"Of course, Hon," she was assertive.

Driving home, Mark suddenly thought of a plan to find out why Shara is always going somewhere on a Friday night, except for only once. Where does she really go? To meet Roland? However, he's been moving away from that thought, considering how she's been acting around him. Then, further thinking, I'm going to hitch a ride in her trunk, to find out once and for all where she was going. The boxes were small, so he knew there was plenty of room to be able to sit.

Chapter 21

Around 6:00pm, on the 12th, Mark parked his car behind a small tree line bordering her house. Unknown to Shara, he knew where she kept the spare car keys. They were underneath a flower pot, because he happened to see her put them there one night when she accidentally locked herself out. So, he quietly stole up to the flower pot, then unlocking the trunk, and returning the keys, except for the trunk key, back to under the pot.

He remembered, she always told him she usually went somewhere around 7:30, after paying her one employee, and locking up. True to her word, crouched behind her car, when she called out to her mother, "I'll be home around midnight."

Quietly and quickly, he got into the trunk, realizing the boxes were gone. Good, he thought, more room. Soon, Shara pulled out to her supposed meeting in Pacerville. Mark could feel how it wasn't long before the car was going down what seemed like a bumpy rural road. Wondering if Pacerville is that rural, when she was taking lots of left and rights. Boy, this buyer must really live in the boondocks.

Finally, after at least an hour, he heard voices, and Shara saying "John, I see a spot by the trees."

The car was stopped then. After a few minutes, he cracked open the trunk. He was lucky she parked against the back of some high shrubs. Then, he could see a façade of doors against an embankment with people going in. Then, like a hammer, it came down on him. People were putting black cloaks and robes on over their clothing. What the hell? What is this place? The next shock came, when Billy and Cindy Lou were walking hand in hand. Then, they quickly donned robes. Oh my God, he thought. This is a devil witchcraft cult that Billy must have gotten into. Shara, all this time must been a witch. I've been used, lied to, and God knows what else. Then, he heard a rumble of a bus, with Connecticut plates, and men and women, mostly in their twenties. They were all headed to the doors, putting on their robes. Then he heard, "Hey Reggie," he could see a tall man approach a black man, putting a cloak of burning flames on him.

"What's up Jack?"

"This damn robe has a tear down the side. Do we have any extras?" "Yeah, in the bus. In the trunk there should be a couple of extras."

Quickly, this Jack guy went into the bus, and slipped on a robe. As soon as he was out of sight, Mark ran into the bus and luck had it, there was one left. Hurrying, as everybody had already passed through the doors, he went over there. A guard stopped him.

"What party are you with?"

"Oh, the Connecticut party. I had to take a mad piss. The damn restroom in the bus is beyond filthy, so I went behind a tree."

"Okay," the guard laughed, "Follow this man," pointing.

He was blindfolded, until he reached the underground, then the man removed it, as he was seated with the Connecticut party. As soon as his eyes focused, he was more in shock, as he trained on the three women sitting up front. It was Shara, and the blonde was Karen, Red's girlfriend. He was overwhelmed in grief, if that was even the right word. Being in the back, and because of the volume of people, he doubted that she saw him. Then, further scanning, he thought he could see Cindy Lou was on an upper tier, as were several other women, wearing, what looked like witches' cloaks and hoods. Then, he thought, somehow, I must get out of here and get back in the trunk before it's over.

A man on his right nudged him softly saying, "This is your first time?" "Yeah," Mark replied.

"My name is Al. I don't remember seeing you on the bus." "Oh," Mark tried to sound convincing, "I was in the back." Before Al could say anything else, Criptin took center stage.

"Welcome my devil worshipers, Welcome! How we are shutting down little by little, the sanctimonious religious lies, that Christ is the savior. We have made great strides in the population, the schools, colleges. Have you noticed, that fewer people are going to church and other places, to falsely pray to a non-existing entity? Have you noticed how the left political agenda has come to the forefront? Putting aside the bible and endorsing the anti-Christ messengers of a corrupt religious ideology? Remember, there's no God, he was disposed of eons ago, by mankind's true ruler of the mass,s Satan. Satan has proved the blasphemy fueled desecration of the murderous hordes of religious wars, that killed millions over the centuries, to fight over a God that doesn't exist. Millions more, tortured and imprisoned, over a God which is just a rallying cause for people like the bloody priests of the inquisition. The pedophile priests of this day, and I could go on and on. You, my friends, know the truth has always come out. For any new people, I am sure you have been told there are plenty of your favorite drugs for the taking, women are ready for fornication. We also have venues for the gay community. There are special rooms for the darker side. For bondage, hard porn, gambling, and everything else. We only request, that everyone shall make a small donation. Behind me, are my three trusted witches. Karen, Shara, and Vivian. Above them are thirty-two other witch disciples. Then, of course on my right is my trusted warlock, Pearl Jam. My security, Red, Vern, and Roland, and then the rest of my staff. So, go now to the food court, the sex dens, the drugs. Enjoy yourselves. Remember, there is no law here."

Mark felt like he was ready to barf. Soon, everybody went off to their choices. Mark pretended he was checking out where he wanted to go and settled in the food court. In taking it all in, he couldn't believe what was unfolding before his eyes. He didn't want to act suspicious, so he went over to the drug den, but the smell nearly bowled him over. Then, he went up to what looked like an ATM. Moving away from that, he opened a door to the goings on in sexual orgies, where several people, were doing everything unimaginable; it was then, he retreated back to the food court. Knowing, he must remain shadowy. Finally, hours later, after more speeches from Criptin and Pearl Jam, the body, for the most part started to disband.

However, Mark didn't know, in some venues like the sex den, they could be an all-night affair. As he was walking out, there was suddenly a shuffle of people, when two guards grabbed him. Then, a short, pudgy man said, "Al, is this the guy?"

At that moment, Red, Roland, and Vern were there, and Roland ripped off Mark's hood.

"This is Mark Martin. He's Shara's new boyfriend."

The pudgy man quickly pointed out that he's the bus driver from the Connecticut bus line, and Al pointed him out and said he was acting suspicious and said he was on the bus, which was a lie. He bounced back and forth, like he was the law or a private eye.

While this was going down, Cindy Lou and Billy were approaching the exit to move up from the cave, when she said, "Hon, let me run back and pee. It's a long ride back, I'll only be a few."

"Okay," Billy nodded, "I'll meet you in the car."

However, as she was ready to leave the restroom, she heard yelling and swearing. Cracking the door open, her heart jumped, as Mark was roughly pushed down the hallway.

Then, racing back, she jumped in the car.

"Oh my God Billy. They've got your brother! You drive, I've got to text Carol." Mark was pushed into Criptin's office. Criptin had a look of defiance.

"Who's this, that upsets the sanctuary of my office?"

Red threw Mark down, "This is Billy Martin's twin brother Mark."

Vern added, "He has been spying on us according to the bus driver, and some Al guy from the Connecticut party."

Criptin instructed Red to bring them up for questioning. After hearing their accounts, he said, "Why are you here Mr. Martin?"

Mark then told him the truth, "To find out where Shara has been going on Friday nights." "That's bullshit," a hot Roland spewed out. "He's probably a plant for the cops."

"Well, it's late," Criptin elaborated, "I've got to get back to the wife and kids."

Then he looked into Mark's eyes, "You're lucky Pearl Jam has already left. He was once an intelligence officer in the Siberian Army, and they don't take lightly to meddling. Tie him in a chair. I'll call Shara to come here in the morning and we will hear what she has to say."

"No!" Mark yelled. "It has nothing to do with her. I hid in the trunk. That's the truth!" "Enough said!" Criptin was livid.

As Billy raced to Cindy Lou's apartment, Cindy Lou in her text to Carol, told her about Mark and that his safety was at risk.

After Criptin left, Mark was gagged and tied hand and foot in the metal chair. Red broke out a deck of cards.

"Let's play five card stud. It's going to be a long night." Vern took a seat, "Where's Roland?"

Then, Roland appeared from a back room holding a nasty whip. "Vern, help me tie him to the crossbeam and get rid of his clothes." Red, then tore into him.

"Are you crazy? Criptin told us to wait for Shara."

"No problem," Roland grinned, "When she comes, he'll be a bloody mess, and I'm sure he will tell us everything when I peel his skin off."

"No!" Red was assertive again. "No fucking way. Now ditch the whip." Roland reluctantly threw it down.

Vern laughed, "Roland buddy, you want revenge for him stealing your girl." "Well, yeah, that's part of it. But Martin is done anyways."

"What do you mean?" Vern questioned.

"Criptin and Pearl Jam have been eying Shara to take the position of the mother witch of all disciples."

"Yea, so what?"

"Are you kidding Vern? Have you ever read the so-called witch manual published? Supposedly by Criptin's father."

Red said, "That's just bull."

"Criptin's old man wanted to solidify his standing before he checked out." "What do you mean?" Vern seemed clueless.

"Cancer got him," Red answered. "What's in the manual Red?"

Roland picked his way past a bound Mark, saying, "The initiation to be a mother witch, means she has to kill somebody."

Punching Mark in the arm and laughing.

"That's never been used before. I'm not sure Criptin would do that." Red put his spin on it.

"I disagree," Roland seemed excited, "I know Criptin wants Shara for mother witch.

Criptin would want her to kill him." Roland then added, "I know she was a witch in Peru, she is a true believer of the Devil."

Then, he walked to the bound Mark laughing, "I think you're red meat Martin." Mark was thrashing in his chair, trying to loosen the bonds.

As morning unfolded, Mark was still bound but not gagged. Only a couple times, he was freed for bathroom breaks, alongside Red, holding a blue plated .45.

Vern checked his watch, "They should be here any time now."

Criptin was the first to arrive. Shortly, Shara, who supposedly didn't know why she was sent for, was a close second. She walked into Criptin's office, seeing Mark tied and gagged, probably sent shock waves through her, but she failed to show any emotions. Criptin then began his venomous spiel, only ending with Martin, who was canvassing the place, and could be working with the cops.

"What do you think Shara?"

Shara focused into the pleading eyes of Mark. "How did he get here?"

Red answered, "Hitched a ride in your trunk."

"To me, he was just another lover that I have used and taken along the sacred path of a disciple."

She looked at Roland, "They are all expendable. I use them, drain their bodies of their insatiable drive, all they cherish in a love, that I scorn; for Satan is the blackened soul of the underworld. Knowing these heathen men, who only strive to populate and perpetuate a tainted vision by the evil clergy and all of the religious zealots."

"Well said!" Criptin laughed at her fake amorous love. At that moment, Pearl Jam joined them.

"Criptin, I have been briefed. I am sure my talent for getting out the truth won't be wasted on him," as he waved a torture instrument with a metal handle, with a diabolical sharp claw.

Criptin smiled, "No Pearl Jam! Shara is going to show her love of Satan, by being our mother witch, and doing so, she will slay the nonbeliever, and it's more rewarding for Satan. For Shara, has manipulated his mind and body. Are you Shara, willing to kill the infidel, to become the mother witch of the inner society?"

"I would be honored great Criptin."

"Excellent Shara. The movement will continue in destroying churches, temples, mosques, and others. For Lucifer will reign supreme. Go now, to my side room where there is a black altar, upside down crucifix, and a bloody host. This is where you will reflect on the Prince of Darkness, and soon will send Mr. Martin to burn in hell."

Shara walked past Mark, ignoring his grunts and pleas.

Criptin walked up to Mark, "Don't take it so bad Mr. Martin. You will be buried on your parent's property in an old abandoned well. So, hang loose. Just look at it this way, you're going home again. So, my friend, before you know it, it will be all over.

Chapter 22

Back at the Martin farm, Rick walked in the kitchen, as Tess was sitting in a chair. "Honey, you look like you've got a convicts headache."

"What's that mean?"

"Someone who is bored."

"No honey not bored. Just reflecting, how when we moved here I thought our two boys would be here now. I never hardly see them."

Rick smiled, "Don't worry Tessie my love. I am sure at some point, they will be bringing their girlfriends here for your awesome breakfasts'. Probably, at this very moment, Mark and Billy are doing whatever their girlfriend gin up; like clubbing like we use to do when I was dating you."

Tess grinned, then said, "Does that include flatarming?" They both went into a tirade of laughter.

Rick saying, "Honey, I don't think flatarming is in their vocabulary."

Meanwhile, at the Devil cult, Criptin instructed Red and Vern to untie Mark, and strap him to a bench.

"Remove his shirt," he further said.

Soon, Mark was fastened to the bench, still gagged. Shara came out of the room looking eager to be elevated to the highest witch. Criptin smiled, it was more like a diabolical smirk.

"Are you Shara, ready for your initiation to be elevated to serve Satan as the head witch of the Rockville chapter of the devil cult?"

"I am ready. In fact, I am more than ready Criptin, master of the Rockville Cult." Criptin had even a greater sinister smile.

Pearl Jam, then passed what looked like a paring knife. Criptin, then bent over Mark, making a small circle incision around Mark's heart area, Mark grimaced in agony. Criptin then opened a small red box and retrieved a red handled dagger with the image of Satan on the side of the glittering blade.

"You, my Shara, will plunge the blade into the circle around his heart. Then you will be the mother of all witches."

Roland looked over in gratification.

Shara took the dagger and raised it high.

Mark, frozen in fear, knew he would be dead within a few seconds.

As Shara brought the dagger down, she suddenly, within the blink of an eye, thrust it upwards, into Criptin's neck. A short scream, then a rapid flow of blood poured out.

Pearl Jam, Red, Roland, and Vern, along with two guards who were there, were beyond shocked. Then suddenly, coming at them, was a small army of police, FBI, DEA, all along with a swat team.

Pearl Jam, and Red ran out to confront them with guns in hand but were quickly buried in a hail of gunfire. Bringing up the rear, was Billy, Cindy Lou, and Carol, and her son the district attorney Rob Sergi. Roland, Vern, and the guards, were quickly handcuffed. As Shara freed Mark, D.A. Sergi looked down at the bloody body. "This must be Criptin."

Mark overwhelmed, said, "Shara turned the dagger on him."

Soon, the whole story came into focus. Shara was playing Criptin.

After Cindy Lou text-ed Carol, she also text ed Shara and told them all how Mark was in extreme danger.

Billy, saw the weeping circle on Mark's chest. "Brother, you really dodged the bullet!"

However, Mark just couldn't believe how Shara was so convincing, he didn't know what to say.

knew.

Shara walked over, "You okay Mark?"

Mark stepped back, although she saved him, she seemed to be different than the Shara he

"Something wrong?" she asked, as the medic tended to his wound.

"Well, yes and no. Roland said you were a witch in Peru. So, it makes me feel that you weren't truthful, although you saved my ass, I can't wrap my head around who you really are," and then he walked away.

In the following weeks, D.A. Sergi and the task force found a mountain of evidence in a safe in one of the access tunnels. Most of the racketeering, which included murder to bank fraud, was exposed. Many cities, like Boston, Providence, New York, Baltimore, and even in Canada, were taken down. D.A. Sergi didn't press charges on Shara for killing Criptin, as she was more than justified in taking him out. However, the golden light that Shara personified in Mark's mind, had faded.

Chapter 23

One afternoon, Cindy Lou went to Shara's salon for a cut.

Shara was contrite, "Cindy, Mark won't answer my calls or texts."

"Yeah," Cindy responded, "I guess he was traumatized by you actually practicing witchcraft in Peru."

"I know Cin, but I was only seventeen. I was easily led down a dark road. I was kind of brainwashed, that Christ was evil, and the gateway to salvation, lied with Satan. But, then I fell in love with him, and I was coming to my senses. Love trumps over evil. I was somehow going to get out of the cult."

Cindy Lou resonated with her, "Believe me Shara, getting out was almost impossible. Criptin had most members hooked on a hateful ideology, plus the devil shit, drugs, and other stuff."

"I know, but the truth is, that I really and deeply am in love with Mark. But, I know he will never trust me again. What can I do?"

Cindy Lou thought for a moment, "I'll see if his brother can find out what's in his head. Maybe there might be hope."

Rick and Tess were mortified about the whole story of Mark nearly being killed, and how his girlfriend saved him. Yet, she was a witch, and how they were going to dispose of his body in the farm's well, that they once had looked for. Billy and Cindy Lou currently, were on the porch.

Rick commented, "Who would have ever thought, a devil cult was here in Rockville?" Although both parents were relieved that Mark was safe, they kind of shunned away from Cindy Lou, like she was tainted with the scars of witchcraft, despite what Billy had said to the contrary.

After Billy left with Cindy Lou, who he was now living with, Rick looked over the wide expenses of the farm.

"Tess honey," he began, "I think we should sell out, and move back to Park City."

"What??" Tess exclaimed. "The farm is your dream."

"Not anymore. This devil shit has taken the wind out of the sails. I don't want to run a farm, knowing that on the property, they were going to kill Mark and throw him out like yesterday's garbage, down a well, where I don't even know where the fuck it is."

Tess then added, "I understand your reasoning. Poor Mark hardly comes out of his room. That Shara girl has really done a number on him."

"You're right," he agreed, "It's like we bought the farm, then found a slew of pit vipers everywhere. Our dream has been crushed, but Tess, I am sure we will find a new adventure." He then kissed her and said, "I'll start looking for a buyer."

The next morning, Mark knew that he couldn't dwell forever on what happened and jumped in his SUV to go to the job site in Park City.

In another part of Park City, at Carol's house, Billy and Cindy Lou piled into her Chevy Tahoe, on their way to have the tattoos removed from Billy's chest and back.

In Rockville, Shara opened the salon, extremely distraught about Mark, and thought, how can I get in his mind to show him, I'm not into witchcraft, and it was just the twisted adolescent mind of a seventeen-year-old teenager. Somehow, someway, I must try!

Carol, Cindy Lou, and Billy stopped at Uncle Max's Bar and Grille on the way back to Carol's.

Taking booth, Carol voiced, "See Billy, I told you it wouldn't be bad. Alex does stellar work in tattooing and removing them."

"Yup," Billy took a deep swallow of gratitude, "You were dead on center. Just a little sore."

heals."

beer."

Cindy Lou, playing with her multifaceted bracelet added, "You will be for a while, until it Billy laughed, "I'm going to push the healing along, with a goblet of cold German draft Carol ordered a slow gin fizz, while Cindy Lou requested a sex on the beach. Then, they all made their choices for lunch.

Chapter 24

It was a cold day in February, when Rick told the family, that a buyer had been found, and they had to vacate the property by April. Or course, most took it as a bitter pill, that because of the events that deep-sixed Rick and Tess's dreams.

Cassie and Carson were getting ready to return to their home, when Cassie looking at the ominous sky commented, "The weatherman is predicting a nor'easter for Thursday."

"Yeah," Rick mirrored her comment, "They are saying it's going to be bad. Fifteen to twenty inches."

Then, looking at Billy, he knew what he wanted, "All right Billy, you and Mark hitch up the plow, and put your Camaro in the barn. The Ford F-350 will get its first test with you driving."

"Awe shit Dad," Mark said, "I wanted first crack." "Don't worry son, there will be other times."

Carson got up from the table looking at his wife, "Are you ready dear?"

Soon, they were heading home back to Park City.

Billy told his father he would take the truck out for a run, to get used to it.

"Yeah, okay Billy. Just be careful. The rig and the plow set me back over sixty grand." Tess looked at Mark saying, "Billy told me you guys are laid off for the winter?"

"Yeah mom, we're going to sign up for unemployment."

The nor'easter hit, with all guns blazing. Blizzard conditions. Raging winds, zero visibility. All the ingredients for a nasty winter storm. Billy was in the truck with Mark, who was riding shot gun. After a couple of hours, they seemed to be losing the battle to keep the long driveway, barns, and house areas free from snow.

"Damn," Billy exhausted from fighting the snow suggested, "Let's go in for coffee." "Good idea," Mark was on board, "This storm is way worse than they predicted."

Tess went outside to the deck to get a notebook she left there, when she came back in, she was covered in snow. Grabbing the coffee pot, it slipped out of her hand smashing onto the floor. "Whoops," she muttered, "That was the last of the coffee."

Billy, in seeing what happened, said, "It's okay mom. Harry's Donuts always stay open for the town plow drivers. Mark and I will get everybody coffee."

Outside, Billy took shotgun, "You drive bother. I'm beat!"

As they headed for Harrys, "Shit!" Billy exclaimed, "Cindy Lou is not picking up her cell."

"Maybe she forgot to charge it," Mark pointed out. "I doubt it. She's a stickler for things like that."

Then Mark suggested, "Why don't we swing by the apartment and check on her."

"I was just going to say that."

They plowed their way into the driveway. Billy bailed out," Be right back."

Inside, he found her extremely sick, of what she told him was girl trouble. Billy alarmingly noticed a lot of blood on the sheet. He quickly called Mark.

"She said it's girl problems, but she's really sick. What should I do? Call the medics?

This happened once before, and she wouldn't go to a doctor."

"Hold on, I'll call mom."

Although Tess isn't that fond of her, she agreed to check on her, for when she was younger, she worked in a woman's clinic as an aide. Mark drove back and picked up his mother bringing her to Cindy Lou. Then he drove to Harry's for coffee, but before that, he decided to drive by Shara's salon. Why? He wasn't sure.

At the salon, he could see her trying to get out of the driveway, and knew she was wasting her time. She would never make it. The storm picked up and the snow was piling up. So, going against his incriminating thoughts, that she's a lying bitch, he drove up, plowing his way in.

Shara jumped out of the car, not knowing what to say.

Mark got right to the point, "I'll make a path with the plow, then I'll put on a chain, and pull you out."

"Oh," she said, "It's you. I thought it was someone from the town."

"They don't plow private driveways," Mark said in an unfriendly tone. She just stood there mystified. Why is he helping her?

Mark then stared at her all bundled up in a red coat, pull over cap, with half boots. When it seemed like a tiny piece of ice between them started to crack. He plowed the area, then pulled her forward with the built-in winch.

He asked, "Are you going home?"

"Yes, I am. Well, thank you for helping me."

"Shara," he suddenly called out, "The roads are too treacherous, I'll give you a lift." "Oh, no. I should be able to make it. It's only five or six miles."

"Well okay, but I don't think that light Buick Regal will."

Then she thought for a few minutes, "Okay, but I hate to put you out." "Hey," Mark half yelled, "I would help anybody in trouble."

As she tried to step in the cab, she was having trouble reaching the upper handle. Mark again, trying to not be too friendly, went around to give her a boost.

"Oh, thank you Mark. This sure is a big truck."

"Actually, it's a one ton, with oversized tires, that's why it sits up so high."

At first, neither one didn't say too much, until he thought to tell her about Cindy Lou. Shara got anguished, "Thank you Mark, I'll give her a call."

As the truck pulled up to her house, he made a couple of passes with the plow quipping, "It will probably be filled in again before morning."

She stepped off the truck, when he asked, "How are you going to get your car back?" Shara brushed some snow of her cap saying, "The storm is supposed to stop tomorrow afternoon. I can get someone to give me a ride." "Well okay, but I can grab you if you want."

"Maybe you shouldn't Mark. I have done you wrong. I don't think it's a good idea." "Are you sure Shara?"

"I am sure Mark."

Then she walked to her house.

Mark then went to Harry's to get the coffee. Then he picked up his mother, who stabilized Cindy Lou.

Chapter 25

Four weeks later, most of the snow was gone, and the March sun was higher, bringing a little warmth to the first few days of Spring. Rick told the twins not to be too anxious to take the plow off.

Saying, "You know New England. Just wait a minute, the weather could change."

Then, Tess gave the twins the news that they had found a new ranch, with three acres of land, on the outskirts of Park City.

Billy piped up, "Garage I hope?"

"Of course, Billy boy," Rick laughed, "Two car!"

That night, as Mark was checking the vitals on his SUV, his mind was in a daydream. Billy walking over said, "Mark? You look like you're in another world."

"Just thinking."

Billy cut him off, "I bet it's about Shara." "Why do you say that?"

"My inclination is, I don't think you're over her. Not by a long shot."

"Wow Billy, big word." Then, he pulled the dipstick out, "Yeah," he confessed, "A little." "After all," Billy continued, "She did save your ass from that monster Criptin. What would have happened if Criptin somehow grabbed her arm and then stabbed you? Red might have shot you and Shara. She took a ballsy chance in saving you. Don't let her get away, no matter what she says."

"Alright Billy, enough! I've got to think."

"Well, excuse me brother Mark," and he went back to the house.

A couple of days went by, and the whole Shara thing was eating at Mark. Then he thought, why don't I drive to the salon for a cut. She does men's hair too. Hey, why the hell not, I can only sink or swim.

Walking in, around 11:00am, only two customers were getting haircuts. Shara did a double take, "Can I help you?"

"Well yeah, I need a haircut."

"Alright, Kaylee my assistant is almost done." Kaylee looked almost like a high school kid.

"Well," Mark was firm, "No disrespect to Kaylee, but I want you to cut me."

Shara looked over, finally saying, "Well okay, but you're going to have to wait a while." Mark was assertive, "I have all day."

Mark could see, the young girl Kaylee was trying to take in the exchange, and the body language.

Finally, he took a seat in the high chair.

As Shara got a comb and trimmer, "How do you want it cut?" "The same, but shorter."

Then she started his hair cut, when Mark yelled out, stunning her. "What's the matter?" She was confused.

"Why are you smashing the razor against my head?"

Her mouth dropped, and she looked at him. He had a shit eating grin on his face. She punched him in the shoulder, "Come on Mark, quit the playing."

"Okay," he kind of smiled.

"Now Mark, why are you here?" "For a haircut."

"Cut to the chase Mark Martin, what do you want?"

"Wow," he took notice of her phrase, "You learned our sayings quick. Well then, I guess I'll cut to the chase! I just wanted to look at your beautiful face." Shara was quiet for a moment or two.

"Mark, I already told you, it would never work out."

"Why?" Mark was dogged, "Because you were a witch in Peru?"

Before she could answer, he said, "Guess what? I don't believe in witches. I wouldn't care if you were Cleopatra's half sister from two thousand years ago. I am in love with you."

Shara grabbed the box of tissues, blotting her eyes.

"Now, Miss Shara Devega, would you mind finishing my hair cut?"

Chapter 26

It was the second week in July, when Cassie and Carson puled into Rick and Tess's new home for a cook out. They were soon followed by Billy and Cindy Lou. Also invited, was Carol Uxbridge and her son the D.A. Rob Sergi, as well as some of Rick and Tess's old and new friends. They were all there, waiting for the newlyweds,

In the distance, the white Ford Edge, was making its arrival. Then, Mark and Shara alighted, giving warm greetings to all.

"So," Carson said, "How does it feel to be married?"

"Couldn't be better," as he introduced Shara to him, and most everybody else that didn't know her.

Tess was preparing a jello mold, when her friend Fay commented, "They make a lovely couple, what a beautiful bride he's got."

"Yeah," Tess agreed, "They just got back from Las Vegas last week. They tied the knot in the same chapel that Elvis got married in."

Fay was pleased, "That's great Tess. You and I were crazy about him!" "Well, I guess Mark loved his music as much as we did."

After the cookout, everybody left except Billy and Cindy Lou, and of course Mark and Shara. Then, around 10:00pm, Mark finished his beer, saying, "It's getting late, so I guess we will be heading back to our apartment in Rockville."

Cindy Lou made Shara aware that her eyeliner was smudged. Shara looked in the mirror in the bathroom, then called out to Mark, "Honey, I left my pocketbook in the car. Would you mind getting it? I need to fix my eyes."

Mark laughed, saying to himself, "Women, and their passions for the perfect look."

He scooted over to the SUV, grabbing the pocketbook, when he didn't see a small hole, and tripped, dumping the contents of it onto the ground.

"Damn," he said.

In the dim light from the lamp post, he started picking up her stuff, when he noticed a small, round, metal object, that came ajar from a side compartment. Pulling it out, it had a hex sign stamped on it. From what now he knows about them, they were used to put an evil spell on things or people. To bewitched!

As Billy and Cindy Lou were heading for their car, they saw Mark bent over, and it looked like he was half crying. Seeing the pocketbook on the ground, with all Shara's things everywhere, Billy quickly said, "Mark, what's wrong?"

Mark looked up, showing him the hex medal. The same symbol, that was once tattooed on his back. Mark then got up, grabbed the medal, and he headed to confront his new wife.

When in the corner of his eye, Billy saw Cindy Lou had a smile on her face.

"What are you smiling about?" "I'm not smiling, not at all." "Well, it looked like it to me."

"It's probably the dim light playing tricks with your eyes."

Billy said, "Well, regardless, I don't want to know what's going to happen next."

As they jumped in the Camaro, and headed back to Rockville, the dark sky hovered over them. It seemed like a sinister mass, that was ready to suck them up.

Printed in the United States
By Bookmasters